Tales from Beyond the Wood

Adrian Farrel

For Linda,

Everytime you read a story
be pleased if it is about you.

Best wishes

This edition published in 2017 by FeedARead.com Publishing

Copyright © Adrian Farrel, 2017

The author asserts his moral right under the Copyright, Designs and Patents Act, 1988, to be identified as the author of this work.

This work is licensed under the
Creative Commons Attribution-NonCommercial-ShareAlike
4.0 International License.

To view a copy of this licence, visit
http://creativecommons.org/licenses/by-nc-sa/4.0

British Library Cataloguing-in-Publication Data
A CIP catalogue record for this title is available on request from the British Library.

Typeset in Candara

For Joshua:
dare to dream

Contents

Introduction	1
How the Owls Made Night	5
The Dragon King's Ghost	9
A Cow for a Lady	13
Tinstaafl Castle	19
The Moon Tree	33
The Wax Crayon	39
The Monk	43
Snow White	53
The Faery Feast	61
The Caring Father	65
The Wise Men of Kulm	71
Seven Swans	79
The Drawing	83
The Tortoise and the Wise Man	97
The Boy Who Flew to a Better Place	101
The Thieving Magpie	113
Mr Christy and Clever Simon	123
The Donkey with Golden Shit	135
The Inn at Chillingford	143
Goodman's Rock	145
Feathers	155
Not Possible	157

Introduction

I didn't start writing fairy stories until after I was fifty, but in the few short years since then I haven't been able to stop. *Tales from Beyond the Wood* is my third collection, this time with twenty-two original tales. The first two stories in this book were completed even before *More Tales from the Wood* had been published, and as this volume goes to the printers I have already completed three stories for the next book, provisionally titled *Tales from the Castle*.

The most frequent questions I am asked are "What age are these stories intended for?" and "What is the inspiration for your tales?"

The first question is easily handled: they are for children of all ages. The language I use is not complex, but the vocabulary is uncompromising. This means that children of eight or nine with solid reading skills should be comfortable, and the stories can, of course, be read to younger children.

But beware! These are not happy-ever-after Disney fairy stories. The endings can be unexpected, and sometimes justice is handed out in a way that adults seem to be uncomfortable about, but that fits well with the expectations of children. If in doubt, I urge you to read the stories first and then pass the books on to your children.

As to the inspiration, that comes from all sorts of places as I read around the subject and digest other collections of tales. I was particularly impressed by a book of folk tales collected by Franz Xaver von Schönwerth in Bavaria in the 1850s (at the same time that the Grimm brothers were working) and published by Penguin in 2015 as *The Turnip Princess: And Other Newly Discovered Fairy*

Tales. Although the translation is a bit rough and ready, and despite the fact that the stories were never edited, this anthology contains enough new material to be exciting for any fairy tale enthusiast. One feature of several stories is their brevity and this triggered me to experiment with my own short tales, giving rise to *Feathers*, *The Inn at Chillingford*, and *The Faery Feast*.

Another book that has inspired me immensely is *Tatterdemalion*, a story written by Sylvia Linsteadt to tie together fourteen exquisite pictures by Rima Staines. This gave rise to *Return to Sender* in *More Tales from the Wood*, and *How the Owls Made Night* in this collection.

I've also been reading and learning about the topic. *Once Upon a Time: A Short History of Fairy Tale* by Marina Warner is highly readable and informative, a must-read for all connoisseurs of the genre. On the other hand, despite being classed as a classic, *Shadow and Evil in Fairy Tales* by Marie-Louise von Franz is not an easy read and is of questionable content. But both books include plenty of examples, and describe a number of archetypes. These led me to *The Caring Father*, *The Moon Tree*, *Tinstaafl Castle*, *Seven Swans*, *The Wise Men of Kulm*, *The Monk*, and *The Donkey with Golden Shit* (which was helped by a description of Italo Calvino's life).

The Tortoise and the Wise Man is obviously a mash-up of the death of Aeschylus and the old Aesop fable, while *The Monk* is based on the story of Saint Anthony, who was led to a poor shoemaker in Alexandria and learned a lesson in piety from him.

A few other tales came to me while musing on some of the traditional folk stories. *Snow White* is an obvious example, although it owes as much to assorted Scandinavian and Northern European stories of ice princesses as it does to the old tale of blood in the snow.

Particular thanks to Ron Bonica for pointing me at the Sicilian tale of the wooden bowl that metamorphosed into *The Wax Crayon*. As for the inspiration for *The Thieving Magpie*, I can only say, "If the cap fits, wear it!"

I hope that the diversity of the stories in this collection will prove enjoyable to all.

How the Owls Made Night

After Chramleigh made the World, after She created the seas, after the storms and the winds were set free, long after the animals had been allowed to roam the planet and swim in the oceans, long even after Chramleigh had lit the stars in the sky, the owls sat in a cherry tree and debated the way their lives had turned out.

It was commonly accepted by most of the animals that the owls were the wisest of the creatures. Of course, the alligators, in their ignorance, were of the opinion that they were pretty much the smartest of all animals. And the sloths didn't have time for thought in their busy days. The cats had their own opinions about who had most knowledge, but they were not about to share their ideas with anyone. And the wrens kept their own council.

In the branches of the tree amongst the bunches of pink flowers the owls sighed. "How," they asked, "could this be called a fair world?" They, unasked-for and against all probability, had been created as carnivores. Not carrion feeders, but hunters. What sort of life was that for one of Chramleigh's creatures?

Being wise was scant compensation. Certainly the owls could work out precisely the most probable routes that voles would take as they scurried from their burrows to the fallen grain heads, or the paths the mice would take as they trotted out in search of moss for their nests. But Chramleigh, in Her wisdom, had set the sun in the sky, and how could the owls hunt when their shadows always gave warning?

So the owls sat and became depressed. "What is the point?" they wondered.

But then they contrived a plan. If the great Chramleigh so loved all Her creations, if She wanted each and every one of them to thrive, if She was truly compassionate, then the owls would test Her. They would challenge Her very essence. They would try Her love. The owls resolved to sit in their tree and watch the sun. They would not hunt, they would not eat, they would not thrive until the beneficent and glorious Chramleigh understood how much She made them suffer. They would hold out until death if necessary to get Her to appreciate how unfair Her world was; until She made their lives a little easier.

And so there they sat. The blossoms swung in the breeze. The mice and voles cavorted unmolested. The sun made its normal circuit in the sky: round and round. The bellies of the owls grew tight. And they watched.

They watched the sun in its orbit as they sat. They tracked it with their large eyes reflecting the glare. They sat quiet and still, just turning their heads as the sun rode on its path across the sky. Slowly, slowly, round and round they turned their heads. A slow rotation of their faces always turned towards the golden stare of the sun. They might have twisted their heads right off if they had not realised just in time that Chramleigh was not, in fact, watching everything, caring for everything.

Thus the owls, the wisest of the creatures, understood that they were responsible for their own welfare. They now knew that if anything was to change in their world it would come through their endeavours and theirs alone.

The first order of business was, of course, to fill their aching bellies. For who amongst us can properly think and be inventive when their stomach cries out for attention?

The little animals of the undergrowth had forgotten their fear while the owls fasted. The scuttling beasts of the grasses and the scurrying creatures of heathland had

How the Owls Made Night

laid aside their timidity and so fell prey to the owls' hunger.

But soon enough the old order was renewed. The mice taught their children, the voles whispered to the shrews: "Beware of the sudden shadow. Have a care for the blot that sweeps across the ground. For at the end of that cool shade is a talon and a sharp beak, and sure as the grain ripens and the seeds fall, if you let the darkness touch you, the next time anyone sees you you will be just a pellet of bone and fur coughed up by an owl."

So, replete, but seeing their old lives returning, the owls formed a conclave, a parliament, a hooting of ideas and arguments at each other from among the cherries that bent the branches with their ripeness.

At last a plot was laid, and after careful consideration and thoughtful incubation, the plan was hatched.

Forty-nine of the largest owls rose together and soaring on their great wings rose into the sky. Higher and higher they flew, now circling, now climbing with powerful thrusts of their muscles.

Closer and ever closer they came to the sun until it seemed to those who remained amongst the fruits on the tree that they must surely catch fire and plunge back to the ground as balls of flaming feathers, or else be swallowed and eaten by that ruddy face.

But finally, arriving at the sun and finding it resolute and unwilling to cease its shining for the convenience of the owls, those forty-nine great birds swooped and swirled, and together drew the feathers of their huge wings across the face of the sun and so cast the world into darkness.

In this new blackness their kith and kin hunted relentlessly and ferociously. Whole families of twitching

How the Owls Made Night

noses were slaughtered. Until, tired from their flight, the forty-nine returned to the cherry tree to sleep.

But every day those same forty-nine great owls take to the sky. The light dims and day turns to dusk as they climb higher and closer to the sun. And then, reaching their target, they spread out the feathers of their wings and night descends once more.

The Dragon King's Ghost

The dragon people live in the wild ocean to the west of the westernmost islands where the winds howl and the waves boil with white crests.

The fishing boats don't go there: the weather is too fierce and the currents too unpredictable. Even the great birds of the sea, the osprey, the auks, and the albatrosses, don't venture to that part of the ocean.

The Dragon King is a terrible sight with his three rows of flashing teeth, his burning eyes of gold and green, and his spiny lashing tail. He is feared by all: the mariners, with their great four-masted ships that ply the trade winds to carry spices and skins and bring home gold and jewels, tell stories of how the king in his rage can break a vessel in two, snapping its keel like the spine of a whale and sending it to the seabed where the drowned crew become food for the fishes. His own people live in terror of his wild and unpredictable temper, and even the ancient fishes of the deep that slide along the dark and stony ocean floor with sightless eyes scouring the eternal blackness, even those fish have learned to keep their distance.

As well as his mighty body with its fierce claws and untarnishable scales, in addition to his fiery breath and the jets of steam with which he can bring down a griffin flying far overhead, on top of the magnificence of his soaring flight, the beating of his four leathery wings, and speed of his dive, the Dragon King has three wonderful weapons that he can wield in defence of his realm and to keep order among his subjects.

First among these weapons is a great bowl of polished jade as green as the water itself and as deep as it is round. The Dragon King can use this bowl to see the future and so that he may lead his warriors to the right

The Dragon King's Ghost

place to meet any challenge or threat. Thus, he has three times vanquished the army of the Monkey Prince, and driven the Ice Lords back to their fastness in the north.

The second of the Dragon King's weapons is Neptune's trident. The King stole this from the god during a great battle many years ago. He wields the trident to call down lightning from the sky and strike any foe on land or sea.

But perhaps the most fearsome weapon is the Dragon King's ghost. He keeps it in a glass bottle: a bottle of deep blue glass cast overboard from a merchant vessel by a sailor both drunk and disappointed; a bottle washed and scoured by the tides so that its surface is criss-crossed by a million scratches and it looks silver when it catches the light; a bottle scavenged from the seabed by the Dragon King and taken back to his lair.

The King keeps the bottle safe and touches it with care. He has sealed its neck with the eyeball of a giant squid that ventured too close one dark winter's night. Not only is this a perfect fit for the opening, an effective airtight, watertight seal, but it allows the Dragon King to keep watch on the bottle and be sure that no one is trying to steal the ghost.

The King has never had to use the ghost in battle. Sometimes, such as when negotiating a peace with the Queen of the Mermaids, he brings out the bottle and holds it delicately between two claws as if to say, "You probably do not want to give me any surprises in this discussion just in case, in my consternation, I become distracted and accidentally drop the bottle or squeeze it too tightly with my talons so that it smashes and the ghost is set free."

The ghost swirls and writhes inside its vitreous prison. Its form is unclear through the scratched glass, but

The Dragon King's Ghost

you can make out the coils of smokey grey and mustard yellow boiling behind the glass walls.

The ghost is angry and frustrated. It is also old and tired. It is sad and lonely. It bitterly regrets the day it went exploring and looked inside the bottle that now imprisons it.

When the Dragon King holds the bottle aloft for emphasis in his negotiations the ghost swirls furiously, frantically. At these times it knows it is closest to release. Should the bottle drop and shatter, or should the Dragon King unstop the neck to let loose a curse upon his enemies, then the ghost stands ready to seize its chance.

And what is the first thing the ghost would do on gaining its freedom?

Would it rush to hide in some forgotten corner? No! It has had enough solitude. And the risk of being trapped for a second time is far too much to bear.

Would it take bloody and terrible revenge on its captor to pay back for all the years? No, not that either. The ghost has never seen its gaoler, never known who saw it sneak into the bottle, never understood how an eyeball suddenly trapped it. The ghost cannot target the Dragon King because it has never heard of his royal majesty.

What then? Will the ghost vent its wrath on all and everyone? Will it wrap tendrils of itself around throats and squeeze? Will it fill lungs with its swirling presence, forcing out air and suffocating life? Will it take the form of a burning lance and pierce-through the hearts of those who stand before it?

No, the ghost will do none of these things for it is only a ghost. When the Dragon King's ghost finally gains its freedom it will do what it should have done all those years ago. It will do what it most regrets not having done

The Dragon King's Ghost

when it could. When it is released, the Dragon King's ghost will dissipate and fade, blending with the wind and becoming as insubstantial as the scent of spring blossoms when autumn frost first arrives. It will, in the way of all ghosts, cease to be.

A Cow for a Lady

Three young men who all came from the same village wanted to impress a certain girl with their prospects in the hope that she might be interested in them and marry the richest.

Now you have to understand that in this village in this part of the country at this time, wealth and security were not measured in gold or precious stones. No, a man might consider himself comfortable if he had enough grain left after the winter to plant a crop for the next year. And a man might think himself well off if he had access to a little land in which to sow his seed.

The first young man was not, in fact, rich. But he knew what it would take: he had heard many people say that to own a cow was a certain route to security, for every year it would bear a calf, and in the intervening months it would yield milk and cheese.

But unfortunately for him, the man did not own a cow and had no way to acquire one. Then, in church one day, he saw a corn dolly and it occurred to him that if he had enough straw he could surely make a cow of his own.

It wasn't easy collecting the straw and storing it so that it wouldn't get wet and rot, but day by day he added to his supply until he had enough to start to model his cow.

The young man was not a skilled artist, but he was determined. Eventually he succeeded in constructing a representation of a cow that met at least his low standards. True, one leg was a little shorter than the others, and the beast sagged in the middle as though its back had been broken by years of carrying heavy loads, but it was enough. He had a cow and he would press his suit.

A Cow for a Lady

"But why would I marry you?" the girl asked. "What can you possibly offer me?"

"I am a wealthy man," he told her. "I may not look rich, but let me tell you, I have a cow. And if you don't believe me, you had better come round and see it for yourself."

Well, this was a fine offer. Imagine the luxury! The girl agreed eagerly and they hurried to where the man lived.

But when they got there, all that they found was a small handful of straw. While the man was away, the cow had got hungry, and seeing a pile of fresh straw it had eaten itself.

"Oh," said the girl, "you are so stupid. I cannot possibly marry you."

* * * * *

The second young man had watched as this story unfolded. For a while he thought he must surely have lost out to his rival, but when he heard how the cow had eaten itself he laughed and laughed.

"Imagine," he chuckled, "the sheer stupidity of it. A cow made of straw!"

But being amused and relieved didn't actually get him any closer to his prize. So he went for a long walk to find inspiration.

In the lane he met an old woman carrying an enormous bundle of willow stems. He stopped her and asked what she had on her back and why.

"I have cut these sticks from the willow trees by the river and I will weave them into baskets that I can sell."

"Tell me," the young man demanded, "do cows eat willow sticks?"

A Cow for a Lady

The old woman looked at him as though he was quite stupid and went on her way.

So the young man thought to himself that if he had enough willow stems, he could surely weave a cow of his own. One that would not eat itself.

It wasn't easy collecting the willow and carrying it back to the house where he lived with his mother. He had to store it under his bed and under the stairs. But day by day he added to his supply until he had enough to start to model his cow.

This young man was not a skilled artist either, but he was determined. Eventually he succeeded in constructing a representation of a cow that met even his low standards. True, it stood a lot higher at the back end than at the front, and it did seem that the beast had three horns, but it was enough. He had a cow and he would press his suit.

"But why would I marry you?" the girl asked. "What can you possibly offer me?"

"I," he told her proudly, "am a wealthy man. You might not think it to look at me, but let me tell you, I have a cow. And if you don't believe me, you had better come round and see it for yourself."

Well, this was still a fine offer. Luxury only to dream of! The girl agreed eagerly and they hurried to where the man lived.

When they got there the man told the girl to look through the window. But their sudden appearance frightened the cow and it backed away from them straight into the fireplace where it burnt up completely until all that was left was a small pile of ashes.

"Oh," said the girl, "you are so stupid. I cannot

A Cow for a Lady

possibly marry you."

* * * * *

Now, the third young man was often considered lazy because he never got around to anything before someone else had done it. But actually, he was careful and thoughtful. He watched and learned.

And what he learned was that the young girl could be impressed with a cow and would be pleased to marry him if he could somehow acquire one. He also learned that straw was too edible and willow too flammable to make a reliable cow.

But that left him no wiser as to what to do. He did not have a cow and he had no way to acquire one. So he sat in the sun on the step of the tiny house he shared with his four sister, three brothers, his parents, and two of his grandparents, and dreamed of cows.

Then, quite suddenly, a cart came past. The poor mule dragging it could hardly make progress, so heavy was the load, and the man who accompanied it had to strike the animal over and over to get it to go forward.

"What have you got there?" called the young man.

"It's a load of bricks to make a new pigsty for the master's pig up at the big house," was the reply.

"Oh, that's interesting," the young man said. "Tell me, do cows eat bricks, and do they burn?"

The man looked at him as though he was quite stupid and went back to beating his mule.

So the young man thought to himself that if he had enough bricks, he could surely make a cow of his own. One that would not eat itself or burn to ashes.

It wasn't easy collecting the bricks. Each one had to be modelled from clay and baked in the fire. He could only

A Cow for a Lady

make one brick each day and put it in the stove after his mother finished cooking dinner in the evening. But day by day he added to his supply until he had enough to start to model his cow.

And this young man was no good at modelling either, but he was determined. Eventually he succeeded in constructing something that he could claim was a cow even though he was not himself convinced. It looked somehow square and rather immobile. But it was enough. He had a cow and he would press his suit.

"But why would I marry you?" the girl asked. "What can you possibly offer me?"

"Some people," he told her proudly, "are full of tall tales about owning cows. I can understand how you would be tired of those people, but let me tell you, I have a cow. And if you don't believe me, you had better come round and see it for yourself."

Well, despite her previous disappointments, this was still a fine offer. And no girl can afford to pass up the opportunity to marry a man with a cow, so the girl agreed eagerly and they hurried to where the man lived.

When they got there the man proudly pointed to the brick-built cow and stood back to await her admiration.

"Oh," said the girl, "you are so stupid. Everyone knows that is not a cow.

"But I will marry you anyway, because with so many fine bricks we shall be able to build a house of our own."

Tinstaafl Castle

A poor farmer had three sons. She was so poor that she only rented the land she worked and had no hopes, no dreams, of having a field of her own. She was so hard up that she never knew how to feed and clothe her children.

High on the hill overlooking the one-room cottage where the family lived stood the ruins of a great fortress called Tinstaafl Castle. Its turrets were broken and jagged: they stood out against the sky like the splintered trunks of forest trees snapped by the storm. Although the tops of the walls were crumbling, they held fast and the castle remained impregnable to all but the elements and the birds. From where they played in the meadow far below, the boys could see the massive oak doors, closed against the world.

Being as they were young lads, the farmer's three sons often talked of how one day they would climb to the castle, find a way through or over the walls, and claim it as their own. Then, each according to his nature, they would become princes leading armies to conquer the world, kings making the folk of the valleys safe against brigands and wild beasts, or benefactors of the arts and the poor.

Their mother tolerated the idle chatter of her boys so long as they did their chores looking after the goat, weeding the turnips, fetching water from the stream, chopping wood, cleaning the cast-iron cook pot, picking rocks from the field to clear the ground and stacking them by the side of the cottage in order to, ultimately, build a new room for when the boys became young men.

But she also warned them about Tinstaafl Castle. She told them tales of the intrepid adventurers who had set off to the castle never to return or, if they did come back, who had been sent mad by what they had seen or what they had not seen. Some had fallen from the wall as

Tinstaafl Castle

they tried to penetrate its fastness. Others had not made it so far and had tumbled from the cliffs as they tried to ascend to the heights where the castle perched. Still more had become lost in the woods as they crossed the valley and climbed towards the cliffs. Many of these starved half to death or came home raving about shadows that spoke to them from the hearts of the trees. These poor souls never had a good night's sleep for the rest of their lives.

And yet, their mother told them on dark winters' nights as the last embers of the fire faded to chill ash, there were also tales of those who had managed to find a way into the castle. Their friends brought word of how they had scaled the walls or reached a window, turning to give a last cheery wave before disappearing forever, for none had ever returned.

* * * * *

One day the farmer's sister died. She had lived in a village two days' walk from the cottage, and her funeral would be held soon. With no time to waste, the farmer gave a few last-minute instructions to her children and set off, leaving them in charge.

Well, the sun had hardly risen before the boys had hatched a plan to visit the castle. With their mother out of the way there was no one to warn them off, or to caution them to be more sensible. So they packed some goat's cheese, gathered some strips of dried turnip, and filled their water bottle. Very soon they were on their way, the oldest leading, and the youngest skipping along behind.

All day they walked, always upwards, and always towards the castle. Now they had to crane their necks to see the stone walls and towers on the cliffs above them.

Tinstaafl Castle

As evening drew in, they reached the edge of the dark forest and made camp for the night. Seated around their fire they shared a simple meal and passed around the water bottle. It was just like home except they had more room to move around.

Soon, one by one, they fell into a deep sleep because they had walked a long way. In the morning they would rise early and make an assault on the castle.

In the dark of the night, before the moon rose, the eldest boy woke with a start and realised a fourth person had joined them around the fire. A tall woman, dressed in grey, sat staring at him, her face deathly pale in the light from the embers.

The boy sat up quickly and politely greeted her.

"You are welcome to share our fire," he said. "Are you cold? I can easily build it up again."

"In truth," she replied, "I am uncommonly chilly. It feels as though the very damp of the ground has seeped into my bones."

So the boy stirred up the embers and dropped some more branches on top. Soon a cheerful blaze sent sparks and embers into the dark sky.

"I knew your mother," the woman said quite suddenly. "In fact, once upon a time I knew her quite well.

"She would not be pleased to know that you are leading the others astray. You are supposed to be the responsible one, but look what danger you are risking."

The boy looked sheepish and defiant at the same time. "I know I am supposed to be in charge," he thought, "and I know the others need me to protect them, and I know our mother expects me to be their leader, but I will not be told what to do by a strange, pale woman whom I have never met before."

Tinstaafl Castle

But out loud he said, "I don't mean to put them in harm's way, but they are quite determined to see the castle up close."

The woman gave him a long grey look, and sighed. "You are so much like you mother: polite, but determined. Since I see you will not be turned aside, let me give you some advice.

"As you make your way to the castle you must pass through the Great Wood. You must not turn from the path whatever good or terrible things you see. If you stay on the track you will come safely through.

"When you reach the castle, go to front door and bang on it with the knocker. As you do this, call out as loud as you can, 'I knock, I bang, I make a din, I ask the Steward to let me in.'

"And then, once you are inside the castle, if you ever want to escape, you must be sure never to touch the mirror."

As the eldest boy pondered this, the heat of the fire warmed his face and he fell back into a deep sleep.

* * * * *

Silvery light flooded the ground around the figures of his sleeping brothers when the middle son woke with a jolt. He, too, quickly became aware of the guest seated beside them, stretching her long pale fingers to the fire for warmth.

Sitting up and yawning, the boy greeted her equally politely. "You look cold," he said, and he started to pile more wood on to the fire without waiting for a reply.

"Are you hungry as well?" he asked. "We don't have much, but I can offer you some strips of turnip. If you chew them a bit, they're not so bad."

Tinstaafl Castle

"You are kind and generous, just like your mother," the woman told him. "I knew her well, long ago. And a piece of dried turnip would be very welcome: it has been several days since I last had food."

As they both sucked on pieces of the leathery root, the visitor gave the boy a long hard look.

"I know I won't convince you to turn back: this adventure is far too exciting for you to resist. So rather than waste my breath (I have so little of it left), let me give you some advice.

"When you have passed through the Great Wood, you will come to a steep rocky area. You must always climb upwards, always take the highest route, never be tempted by the easier path, keep on climbing.

"And when you reach the castle, go to the front door and bang the knocker as hard as you can. Then cry out in your loudest voice, 'Steward do your job once more, draw back the bolt, unlock the lock, release the chain, unbar the door.'

"And finally, when you gain access to the castle, if you ever want to see the light of day again, you must not eat the food."

While the boy considered these words he drifted off to sleep and before long he was snoring soundly.

* * * * *

In the darkest hour, just before dawn, the youngest boy awoke. The fire had gone out and it was so black that he couldn't even see the tip of his own nose. Yet he knew instinctively that there was someone sitting beside him.

"Who is there?" he asked, his voice trembling with fear. "Have you come to harm us? Are my brothers all right?"

Tinstaafl Castle

"Don't fret yourself," came the reply. A woman's voice, but dry and hoarse. "You have nothing to be frightened of. I knew your mother long before you were born and I helped to bring you into this world. I don't intend chasing you out of it."

"You sound parched," said the young boy. "Can I offer you a drink?" And he held the bottle of water out in the darkness.

"That is so kind of you," the voice rasped. "I feel as dry as dust, as arid as the grave. I think I could drink a river."

Cold, bony fingers brushed his as the flask was taken from his hand.

After a long drink, the woman sighed and said, "It has been a long night, and we must all be brave. You follow your brothers faithfully, but don't let them lead you astray. Let me give you some advice to help you on your way.

"Although you want to be as big as your brothers, and even though it frustrates you not to be able to do things for yourself, never be too proud to accept help from your brothers.

"And when you get to the castle, and if you want to get in, you must bang on the door with the big iron knocker and cry out in your loudest voice, 'I am not scared, I will not hide, Steward, now, let me inside!'

"And if you do go into the castle and if you want to escape afterwards, you must remember that you may only bring back one thing."

It was now too late for the young boy to go back to sleep. As the day dawned he set off to find a stream from which to fill the water bottle. When he returned, the grey

Tinstaafl Castle

woman had vanished, fading with the light of day.

* * * * *

It seemed to each boy that he had had a strange dream, but as they walked into the Great Wood they exchanged their stories of the night visitor and they were amazed at how many details of the woman they could each recall. Only the things she had said to each of them were different.

After discussing it a bit, and as the mysterious darkness of the forest enfolded them, they realised their visitor had been their mother's sister: dead, buried, and sitting by their side at the edge of the wood.

As if the shadows of the wood weren't scary enough, this realisation left the boys in a nervous state. They jumped at every noise, and each gnarled old tree seemed to take on the shape of some monster or evil spirit.

The younger two were so terrified that they kept wanting to run off and hide. Each new fright made them leap in the opposite direction. Only their big brother's stern admonitions to stay on the path saved them from getting lost, and soon they came out from between the trees and stared up at the castle on the cliffs above them.

The way forward was not easy. Large boulders were scattered everywhere, and the path seemed to climb outrageously straight up towards the sheerest cliff. The eldest boy wanted to walk along parallel to the face until they could find an easier way. The youngest said they should weave between the massive boulders and rocks, rather than try to climb over them. But, recalling what he had been told, the middle brother insisted that they set

Tinstaafl Castle

their sights on the castle and follow the most direct path.

* * * * *

When they reached the castle they could look out at the world laid out below them. There was the Great Wood, dark and green and stretching on for ever. And way out there, beyond the trees and across the fields, they could just make out their tiny cottage. And far, far away in the furthest distance was the cluster of tiny houses that was the village where their mother's sister was buried.

But they were here for the castle and now they stood before its great oak doors. Just within reach of the oldest boy was a heavy knocker in the shape of a dragon. Its teeth were bared and its tail wrapped around the hinge. The boy reached for it and even though it squirmed and flapped its wings beneath his hand he struck it three times against the door, crying out the lines the woman had told him.

"I knock, I bang, I make a din, I ask the Steward to let me in."

At once the doors swung open and the boy entered in. His brothers sat down in the sunshine to await his return.

Inside the castle was a long corridor with many doorways leading off it. In the first room there was nothing except a bed. In the second room there were some fine chairs that looked very comfortable. In the next room there stood a tall mirror and its reflection showed the boy wearing fine clothes and a green hat with a feather. He was just reaching out to touch the garments when he recalled what he had been told and pulled back his hand.

The next room was a library and f
but in the room after that was a table la
manner of food. There were things that
heard about in tales, such as roast ham
white bread. There were delicacies tha
dreamt of, like glacéed figs and sugar mice. And there were bowls and plates of all of his favourite foods including roast potatoes, buttered parsnips, and mashed carrot. The smell was enticing, but the boy remembered what he had been told and moved on.

In the next room there were musical instruments: a piano with a violin resting on it, a harp standing proudly in a corner, and several bass drums and a tambour lying on a table. These were of no interest to the boy at all, but in the room that followed there was a washstand and next to it, on a table, was a gold brush and a silver comb.

The boy thought he had probably been in the castle quite long enough and did not want to tempt fate. So he picked up the brush, weighed it in his hand, stuffed it inside his jacket and ran back down the passageway.

As he approached daylight he saw that the doors were swinging shut, but he just managed to jump through before they slammed closed behind him.

After the brothers had admired the gold brush, it was the turn of the middle brother. He couldn't reach the knocker even when he stood on tiptoe, but he leapt up and grabbed it even though the dragon snapped its teeth.

Banging as hard as he could, the lad shouted out the verse he had been taught, calling on the Steward to open the door. "Steward do your job once more, draw back the bolt, unlock the lock, release the chain, unbar the door."

Just as before, the great doors swung silently open and the boy slipped inside. The rooms were just how his brother had reported. He avoided touching his reflection even though the dog he saw by his side seemed to cry out to be patted. He just managed to stop himself from eating any food although he was terribly hungry. And in the washroom he rejected the silver comb because he wanted to bring back something even more splendid than his brother's gold brush.

The next room was full of clocks. They ticked and chimed and whirred. And in the following room stood a number of tailor's dummies, each displaying one garment or another. There were ball gowns and wedding dresses, waistcoats and frock coats, but what attracted his attention was a splendid velvet cloak all of black, so dark that it seemed to absorb all the light.

The boy tried it on and, since it fitted him perfectly, he decided to take it and he ran back towards the outside world. As he got near, he saw the doors were closing and only a small gap remained. But he made a dash and squeezed through just as they crashed shut.

He sat outside with his brothers, panting, and told them everything he had seen while they fingered his cloak and admired how it swallowed the sunlight and made him almost invisible.

Well, now it was the turn of the littlest boy. He stretched as high as he could, but the knocker was out of his reach.

"Let me lift you up," said his biggest brother.

But the young lad wouldn't let him. "I can do it myself," he cried.

He jumped and reached for the knocker, but still the dragon eluded him.

"I'll help," offered the middle brother. But the small boy refused him angrily.

Tinstaafl Castle

He ran and leapt. He sprinted and sprang. He wore himself out carrying rocks to make a pile to stand on. But still he couldn't touch the knocker, although the dragon did once lash out with its tail and scratch the boy's knuckles.

At last, collapsing with a sob, exhausted, he remembered what his dead aunt had told him. "All right," he conceded, "you can help me.

"Please," he added in a little voice.

His brothers lifted him up and he knocked loudly and repeated the lines he had been told.

"I am not scared, I will not hide, Steward, now, let me inside!"

The doors swung open and in he went.

The boy wandered from room to room randomly. He touched and played with things as he went. In the music room he ran his fingers across the strings of the harp and heard the sweet music and people laughing, and he rapped on one of the drums and saw soldiers marching. In the library he pulled books from the shelves and laughed as the words wriggled and struggled to get free from the pages. In the room with chairs he sat on the largest most comfortable one and watched the other people around him chatter. He crept out of the bedroom so as not to wake the beautiful lady sleeping there.

In the room with the mirror he admired his reflection and the red robes he wore. He reached out and touched the gold crown on his head, just to make sure it was real.

In the washroom he ran the comb through his hair, and in the clock room he watched the footman wind each clock in turn, sticking a little key into the faces and turning it sharply.

Tinstaafl Castle

When he reached the banquet room, the boy couldn't believe his eyes. He ate candy and chicken, soup and fresh peaches, red cheese and brown chocolate. He crammed his face full of food and left with his pockets full of apples and nuts.

In the tailor's room he tried on a series of hats until he selected a red beret. The next room was an armoury and the boy selected a dagger in a leather sheath with a belt that he strapped around his waist.

And then he was in the treasure room. The boy selected the biggest golden goblet he could carry and filled it to the brim with gemstones and gold coins, with necklaces and rings, with pearls and pendants. Then, struggling under the weight of it all, he made his way back along the corridor.

The door at the end stood wide open. He could see the sun warming the rocks outside, and he could hear his brothers' voices. And then, when he had only two or three paces to go, the doors crashed closed, shutting out all light and leaving a deafening boom echoing around the cold and empty rooms.

He scratched at the door. He pulled at the hinges. He tried to prise the bolt loose. But there was nothing for it, he would have to spend the night inside, for as hard as he banged his fists on the doors and as loud as he shouted he could not make them move. He could not even hear his brothers' voices any more. So he made a bed for himself right up against the doors and went to sleep, to dream of his mother and brothers, their goat, and the little cottage where they all lived.

In the morning he was woken by the steward who told him he was now the king. The castle and everything in it now belonged to him. And so did the land as far as he could see from the highest tower.

Tinstaafl Castle

Fires blazed in the grates and candles lit the way. He could come and go whenever he wanted, and a trumpeter blew a fanfare whenever he passed through the door.

The Moon Tree

Pedro loved fruit. And he couldn't wait. If he saw fruit he had to have it. He didn't care where it was, he just had to taste it.

Pedro was the scourge of fruit shops. If they set up a display of the new season's strawberries or oranges from across the ocean, they had to post a sentry because otherwise Pedro would be found grazing or else seen running away clutching a pineapple.

And every year since Pedro had been able to reach the lowest branches, he would be found hidden amongst the leaves of one tree or another in some angry farmer's orchard. First in the cherry trees, then in the peaches and apricots, and as autumn came on he would be up the apple and pear trees stuffing his pockets and face in equal measure.

So, as you might expect, Pedro was always in trouble. His parents loved him and tried to put him right. They started with stern reprimands, moved on to the removal of privileges, and escalated to making the boy labour in the fields to pay back for what he had taken. And after Pedro's last escapade, when he had taken a tray of raspberries from the Marquesa's kitchen table, his father had promised him a sound thrashing if he was ever caught again.

And now Pedro was running across the fields as fast as his engorged belly would allow him, his hands and face covered in plum juice, and his ears ringing with the shouts and curses of old Domingo. This time Pedro didn't know where to run to. Home was not an option for a few days, at least until everyone had calmed down. He reckoned that his father was probably serious this time, and Pedro had no desire to find out what a leather belt could do to his backside. So he kept running over the fields, across the moor, and into the wood. Here he stopped, sat down at the base of a tree, and looked back towards his home town.

Was that Domingo he could see stomping up the lane towards his home? Was that his father standing at the door waiting to hear news of his son's latest misdemeanours? If he could see them, could they see him where he sat?

Pedro withdrew into the shadows of the forest and idly followed the paths that led deeper into the gloom. Here it might just as easily have been evening, so dim was the light and so cool and musty the air. Pedro was not able to track the passing time except by the weariness that crept into his legs and the empty feeling he started to get in his tummy.

And it was at about this time that Pedro realised he was lost. Each turn he made only seemed to take him deeper into the woods. The paths became less and less well defined, and before long he was just stumbling across the forest floor between the trees without even a track to turn back upon.

Finally, too tired to go forwards or back, Pedro lay down on a bed of leaves and ferns, resolving to sleep and dream of fruit.

* * * * *

Waking some time later, Pedro understood it was now really night. The darkness was complete and suffocating, and the air was much cooler and somewhat damp. His stomach complained, and he recalled his dream of fresh figs and melon slices.

The Moon Tree

He set off walking again as boldly as he dared, placing his feet carefully and reaching out to touch the trunks of trees to steady himself as he went.

How long did he wander for? It seemed like hours to Pedro, but finally he thought he saw a glimmer of light ahead. Was it his father searching for him with a lantern? Or at least the hearth-light from a woodsman's cottage? Or, horror, a witch's shack?

With mixed feelings Pedro shuffled towards the light. It was silvery, not the warm glow of firelight he'd been hoping for. And at last Pedro found himself at the foot of a tree. It had smooth, smooth bark and long, slender leaves that looked pale or silver grey in the light that radiated from a few large fruits shining where they hung on the boughs.

Without further invitation, Pedro started to clamber up the trunk and work his way out along a branch. The fruit he was after seemed the most accessible, but he now realised it was right at the whippy end of the branch and he was forced to worm his way out clasping the tree with his knees and stretching his hands out to grab the fruit. It was rough to the touch and strangely cool. Plucking it, Pedro brought it quickly to his hungry mouth and bit out a huge mouthful.

All the light went out, and Pedro fell out of the tree.

It was completely dark. Pedro lay on the forest floor, bruised but otherwise unhurt. In his left hand he still clutched the silver fruit, but it no longer shone and Pedro could not see it even when he waved it in front of his nose. In his mouth there was an odd taste of cheese.

From out of the darkness came a voice as soft as the rustling of leaves in a light wind, and smooth as the bark of the tree he had climbed, and unbending as the trunk of a great oak.

The Moon Tree

"That was not the act of a friend," it said.

Pedro cowered on the ground and trembled. He had never been happy in the dark and his mind quickly shaped a picture of the monster that was speaking.

"The fruit you stole belonged to me," it said. "The light it gave was for your benefit when you were lost in the dark. And I had almost decided to give you one of the fruits to take to light your way home."

"Oh, please," cried Pedro. "Please give me a light so I can see you and find my way out of the forest."

"Are you sure you want to see me?" asked the voice. "Wouldn't you be happier to hide in the dark?"

"But I want to go home," Pedro whined. "Maybe I could outrun you if I had a light to see by."

"It is possible that you could," said his tormenter. "It has been many years since I ran through the woods chasing anyone.

"I am pleased to hear that you want to return home and face your punishment for stealing those plums," the voice continued. "But I still don't think I should give you a fruit to light your way. You see, I cannot trust you. I think you will eat it sooner or later, and certainly before you are halfway out of the forest."

"No, no!" exclaimed Pedro. "I've learnt my lesson. I'm a reformed character. I will never eat anyone else's fruit ever again."

"I'd like to believe you, but I don't," said the voice. "But I also don't want you hanging around here whimpering and snivelling, disturbing the birds and frightening the trees. So I will make a deal with you.

"You will promise never to steal again, and I will set one of my fruits high up on the tip of the longest branch far up in the sky to light your way. I will place it right up

The Moon Tree

above the clouds, so that no matter how you stretch or what you climb you will never be able to reach it.

"But you will forget your promise, I fear. You are a child and easily distracted by each new fruit you see. So as a reminder, as the days progress, I will take bites from the fruit and it will gradually diminish and wane until there is nothing left and the night is dark. Then you will remember what it is like now in the forest alone in the blackness. But then, and only if you have kept your word, and only if you have genuinely not broken your promise, I will bring the light back piece by piece until you see my face looking down on you from the sky."

When Pedro reached his home, the moon shone brightly, lighting his way up the path to the door where his parent stood waiting anxiously. His father was, of course, too pleased to see him to consider flogging him on account of the plums.

The Wax Crayon

A poet lived with son, his son's wife, and his grandson in a small house at the edge of the town. They had a patch of land with an apple tree and space to grow a few vegetables. There was also a little wooden shed where the poet had retreated to write his poems when he was a younger man.

Of course, poets do not usually become rich through selling their verses or reading out loud to gatherings of awestruck patrons. And so this man took in work writing letters and transcribing documents and contracts for the tradespeople of the town. The son was also trained in the skills of penmanship and together they ran a successful business that put food on the table. And in his turn, the son strove to be a poet while the grandson was learning his letters and might, one day, also join the family trade.

As the years passed, the poet's hands grew stiff with arthritis and he held his pen with more difficulty. He wrote more slowly and took frequent breaks to rest his fingers. His script became less clear and his son adopted the role of chief calligrapher in the partnership, while the poet performed the more mundane work for less affluent clients.

One day, the father and son sat facing each other across the work desk. The old man was transcribing a ledger in black and red. The younger man was just finishing a month-long project of an illuminated manuscript on parchment with gold lettering highlighted in sky blue and emerald green, and tiny figures dancing through the text and sitting around the capital letters looking up at them as though in wonder.

The father, finding his black inkwell empty, reached across the desk for the full bottle. At full stretch he

The Wax Crayon

discovered that the bottle was heavier than he remembered and his hand less strong. The frail fingers spasmed and twisted, the bottled slipped and, to cut a long story short, the whole vessel was emptied across the desk, flooding the ledger and the parchment. Not only was a month's work lost, but the expensive materials were wasted.

Of course the old man was as upset as his son was furious. No one is happy as their capabilities fail, and the man looked back at his previous triumphs with their fine pen-work and delicate lines, and compared them sadly to his latest work, which invariably had wobbly characters and the occasional blot. So when his son took away his nibs and inks and supplied him with a set of pencils of different colours, the father understood his new role.

Once it has started, ageing usually continues. So the old man lost more of his faculties. His eyesight faded so he could only work in the brightest light and, since his son did not trust him with candles, this meant he was limited to a few hours in the middle of the day. His personal hygiene suffered and he began to stink. And he snored all night, and quite a lot of the day.

The son offered little objection when his wife suggested that the one-time poet should move out to the little hut in the garden. Her father-in-law could continue to work at a desk there, and she would be happy, she said, to carry his meals out to him. She comforted him by hoping that he might find time once again to return to writing poems.

Now the old man found that he would drop his pencils or break them by pressing too hard. What is more, he found it difficult to hold a pencil steady and firm while running a knife across it to sharpen the point. He had to shout out for help or shuffle across the garden to knock

The Wax Crayon

on the back door. His son resented the interruptions to his work and didn't like to be reminded of his father's increasing fragility. He made it his own son's responsibility to attend to the supply of pencils and to keep them sharp. But when the boy was at school there was nothing for it but for the man to carefully blot his work, dust it with sand, clean his nib and then walk out into the garden to attend to his father's writing materials. And as it got colder in the twilight days of the year, the man stood out in the rain and snow sharpening pencils and cursing: the hut was too small for two people, and besides, it stank of old man and half-eaten cabbage soup.

The solution that suggested itself was to replace the pot of pencils with a crayon made of wax. This did not need to be sharpened and could be used to work endlessly on those poems which the old man agonised over but which, it now seemed to his son, had probably never been very good at all.

At last, in the springtime when the apple tree was clouded with white and pink blossoms, the old man went to compose his verses in a better place. After the funeral at which a number of poems from his youth were read out, and during which the poet was placed in the earth, the son and grandson returned home. They decided to clean out the hut in the garden and make it into a den for the boy, where he could practise his own drawings and lettering.

Working together they dragged out the old desk, the foetid mattress, and the few worn possessions. They built a fire to consume these reminders, and on to it they tossed the wooden bowl that the old man had eaten from and his piles of paper coated in wax scrawls – the barely legible writings of a poet who had lost the thread of his life. As his father emptied the last box of belongings on to

The Wax Crayon

the flames, the young boy darted forward and grabbed the wax crayon before it could melt or burn.

"What do you want with that old crayon?" his father asked him. "You have a new set of pens that I bought you for Christmas."

"I think it will be useful one day," the boy replied.

"Really?" scoffed the man. "That was your grandfather's crayon. He only used it when he was too old and frail and stupid to use a proper pen and when he couldn't even sharpen his own pencils. It is a thing for an old man."

"Exactly," his son told him. "As I said, I think I will find a use for it one day when you are old."

The Monk

There was once a monk, not old but approaching old age. He spent his days at a monastery in a quiet spot in the foothills of the great mountains. There the younger monks worked the fields, tended the animals, made cheese, cut firewood, cooked, and cleaned. In short, the novices and junior monks did all that was necessary to support the life of the community while the older monks prayed, meditated, or dozed in the sun in the summer and in front of the fire in the winter.

Monastery life was not luxurious, but it was comfortable and safe. No belly went unfilled unless it was on account of a deliberate fast. And no soul went unprayed for.

This monk was commonly held to be wise, and many people came to consult him. Although the monk rarely gave direct advice about a specific issue, he was always thoughtful and considerate, and somehow those who listened to him carefully always found that things worked out for the best.

For the monk was very learned in the scriptures of the monastery and the folklore of the people. When he had listened at length (sometimes at very great length) to the woes of his visitor, nodding to show his attention to detail, tutting when appropriate, sighing when the story was too sad, and patting a knee when the tears flowed, the monk usually started by asking, "And what do you think you should do?" or, "How would you really like this to end up?"

As often as not the monk didn't need to do much more than this. He listened to the troubles, he let his visitors talk, and he gave his consent to the plan of action that his guests proposed.

The Monk

Sometimes it was necessary for the monk to steer the conversation a little by asking, "Do you think that would be wise?" or, "Can you say that that would really be for the best?" And it was only when the supplicant was completely unable to answer their own question that the monk had to offer guidance of his own.

At these times the monk would fall silent and stare into the distance of the far hills or the leaping flames, according to the season. Or he might suggest a meditative stroll in the gardens among the beds of cabbages and roses.

Only after a long and quiet period of thought would the monk offer his opinion. He would usually quote some passage from scripture or a religious text. For example, he might observe, "It is written in our holiest book that a man shall not be better than an ox if he does not keep his stall clean, and yet an ox that walks in the furrow in front of the plough is thrice more blessed than the pond turtle that only basks in the sun."

His visitor would greet such pronouncements with solemnity. When such a holy man gives advice, you do not ask, "What does that mean?" but you search for understanding so as not to seem foolish or devoid of spirituality.

Thus, when rewarded for her long silent wait with exactly this quote, the clockmaker's wife who had complained that she feared her husband's eye was too easily turned by a pretty face and who, she thought, quite probably had wandering hands, thought hard and fast before answering, "Oh, I see! You are so wise. How can I thank you enough? You are right. I must make time for my husband. I must be the counterbalance to his temperament and try not to be so tightly sprung. And that

The Monk

will be the key that keeps our relationship wound and ticking."

And so she departed, telling all whom she met of the saint in the monastery, and returned to her home to love her husband, take an interest in his work, and bear his children.

* * * * *

One day, as the monk took a digestive wander among the late-fruiting apple trees in the sloping, south-facing orchard next to the kitchen garden, the lazy, pollen-laden bees stumbling from autumn flower to autumn flower and the wasps drunk on overripe fruit buzzing angrily at each other, a rat stopped what it was doing and regarded the monk through yellowed, squinting eyes.

He waved his stick at the creature, but instead of scampering away, the rat put down the apple it had been carrying and sat up on its haunches to get a better look at the saint.

"I wonder how it is you have become so saintly. Did God grant you that, or have you made more of yourself than other men have?

"I think you are only pious because you are comfortable. You only pray because you have time to pray. The food in your stomach is the luxury that buys your devotion, and the straw of your mattress is the nest for your dutiful meditations: it is where your thoughts rest themselves before they launch from your mouth as wise platitudes.

"It is true that you know all of the spiritual texts back to front. You probably know them sideways, too. But that is only because the library is rich with vellum and your youth was rich with hours in which to study.

The Monk

"But for all your humble and God-fearing ways, I know of one who lives less than a day's walk from here who is ten times more saintly than you."

The monk was perturbed. He was not used to being addressed thus. None had questioned his saintliness for many years, and although he was neither vain nor ambitious, the monk had quite accepted that he was truly wise and deeply saintly. In his humility he strove each day to be more worthy of these descriptions and prayed harder and listened to his visitors with more care and compassion.

"That is an astounding claim," he told the rat. "Will you not lead me there so that I may meet this paragon and pray at his side?"

"That I will not," said the rat. "My legs are too short and I would tire myself out in no time. But if you place me on your shoulder I will eat this apple as you carry me, and I will also give you directions."

And so they set out: the monk striding carefully, tapping the ground with his stick, and remembering long-since read words from a dusty manuscript on the progression of the soul towards endless light; the rat nibbling at its apple, sucking on the monk's hair where it poked out from under his cap, and occasionally whispering directions or criticisms into the monk's ear.

Arriving at the town as the light was fading, the rat gave instructions: left here, right at the baker's shop, straight past the gallows with its dancing man. A wave to a cousin near the grain store. Duck down close to monk's neck when the ravens look up from their feast on gallows fruit.

With each new street the monk let his eyes run over the crowd. Did these people look holy? No, they looked dirty, preoccupied with life and food and money,

The Monk

unlearned, and unconcerned with their souls or the worship of God.

"How can there be a saint here?" he asked the rat. "All I see is spiritual poverty."

"Just wait," the rat told him. "We will get there."

In the next street an old beggar sat against a wall, his head bowed, his footless legs stretched out toward the gutter.

"Is that the saint?" asked the monk. "Does he sit in prayer?"

"No," the rat replied, "he is a professional beggar who has sawn off his own feet to better attract sympathy and earn more from passers-by. He has a good home, nice food, a wife and children: this is just how he chooses to earn a living."

The monk halted himself in the act of dropping a few coins into the old man's tin cup and moved on.

Around the corner they encountered a man leading two young children by the hand. He spoke soft words to the infants and smiled to dry their tears.

The monk's own mouth crinkled to a smile at this sight.

"What a kind and gentle man," he said, "to care so well for those children and to comfort them thus. Is he the saint?"

"Nothing," remarked the rat, "is ever quite what it seems. That man buys and sells children. He has probably just taken them from their home and will get a better price for them if he can stop their howling."

"It appears to me that this town is quite a pit of iniquity," the monk sighed. "Bring me to the saint so that I may say my prayers and return home."

They passed through a market and halted at a stall selling vegetables. There, an old woman in rags pleaded

The Monk

with the barrow-man for a few damaged and discarded roots. She cried that her housebound husband was starving and that she would make him some broth, but she had no money.

"No money?" smiled the stallholder. "Always with you it is no money. And always I find a few things to let you have." And he handed her an armful of foul and rotting turnips.

"That is true kindness," the monk exclaimed. "Is this the saintly man?"

"Oh, no!" laughed the rat. "That was just a business deal. The greengrocer will take his washing to the old woman later and she will have to wash it for free, a service worth far more than those stinking vegetables. And so, by this means, the woman is kept in poverty and must return time and again to beg for food and provide her services for no money. That man is certainly no saint."

"Well, come on then," exclaimed the monk. "Lead me to the real saint."

The rat directed the monk into a narrow alley, and they followed a well-dressed gentleman down some stone steps. Suddenly, a tile from one of the roofs fell from above with a slight whizzing sound and crashed on to the man's shoulder. He fell to the ground crying out in pain. Almost immediately a young girl ran from a doorway to help. She propped the man up on a bundle of cloths and checked his wound.

"Don't worry," she told him. "You will be comfortable here and I will run to fetch a doctor. He is a friend and will come at once. He will probably even waive his fee as he owes me a favour."

She checked again that the gentleman was as comfortable as possible and then ran off up the passage in the direction from which the monk had come.

The Monk

"That was a true and charitable act," said the monk to the rat. "Is this the saint you have brought me to see?"

"Well," the rant sniggered, "it could seem that way. And it is true that the girl has a man friend who knows her well. He was the man who threw the tile from the rooftop. I should imagine they are both far away by now sharing out the contents of the gentleman's purse that she lifted from him while pretending to check his injuries.

"Let's move on so we don't get caught up in the crowd that comes out to strip this man of his fine clothes."

At the end of the alley it was dark. It would have been dark here even if night was not falling. The setting sun only aided the shadows and added a touch of chill to the damp cold between the walls.

The rat directed the monk down some more steps into a basement. There was no door in the frame, and no light in the room. The grate stood cold, and there was no sound.

The monk stood quietly and waited. He muttered a few of his favourite prayers to stave off the blackness.

Gradually he became aware of some sounds in the darkness. A soft sobbing, some rustling and snuffling, and then a baby began to cry.

A young child's voice spoke up and the sobbing stopped.

"Don't cry, little one. Mummy will be home soon. It must be night by now and she always manages to see us for a few hours. Perhaps she will have some food with her this time. I do hope so. Why don't you hold my hand and go back to sleep?"

"What is this?" breathed the monk to the rat on his shoulder. "What depravity would make a mother neglect her children like this? How can they live in these circumstances?"

But the rat's reply was cut short by the sound of feet on the steps.

"Darlings, are you there? I'm home," came the cry.

And, "Mummy!" shrilled the young voice while the baby also called out.

"Oh, but I'm tired," said the young mother entering the pitch-black basement. "I wish I did not have to work so hard and for so long. I wish I could stay home with you more. But needs must, and today I have bread for you and some sticks for a fire."

There were sounds as the woman moved around in the familiar darkness, touching her children and feeding them. And then a soft light as flames sprung up in the fireplace.

The monk withdrew to the deepest shadows and watched the family huddle round the meagre fire. He saw the child, perhaps three years old, dressed in rags with a dirty face, clutching its piece of bread like a precious treasure. He turned his sad eyes to the baby, now no longer crying, swaddled in dirty cloths and held tight to the breast of a slim and hunched woman, her hair grey, her face lined.

"Don't be fooled," whispered the rat, "into thinking this an old crone. This mother is still young, but her cares and her labour have worn her down. She must leave before first light to start her first job cleaning floors in some merchant's house, before she takes up a broom to sweep the town square. Then, around midday, she heads to the town walls where she is lucky enough to have a job carrying stones for the repair work. This keeps her occupied until late afternoon, when she scrubs pots at the inn."

The Monk

The monk gazed at the family: all three were now asleep in front of the fire.

"In return for her labour," the rat continued, "this young woman earns just enough to pay the rent on this squalid basement. And some days she is able to buy food and fuel for the family.

"On her own she might find a husband and together they could pool their resources. Or she might sleep on the streets until she had saved enough to better herself. But she loves her children and puts them first. So she works herself into premature old age to give them shelter, food, and warmth.

"This, then, is the saintly person of whom I spoke."

The monk was on his knees in prayer. Tears stood on his cheeks.

When the woman woke in the morning, before dawn, she found a purse of gold coins tucked in with the baby at her chest.

And back at the monastery the monk's understanding of holiness had improved. He gave all that he owned to benefit the poor and worked each day tending to the needs of all who came to him. He fed and clothed, and he nursed the sick. He had no time for prayer or contemplation, but he found his life more rewarding, and he knew he was doing God's work.

Snow White

A couple had always wanted a child, but fate was not kind to them. When they were first married they loved only each other. Then when they thought of a child they found they needed a little more money before they could hope to rear an infant. Then they were so tired from their labours that they forgot to dream of a child. And then, suddenly, they were too old.

But they still wished for a child. Now more than ever. But what could they do?

They sat in the afternoon of their lives with all that they needed, but nothing that they wanted. What did it profit them that they had apple trees and a view from their porch? What comfort was it that they had food on the table and fire in the grate? They lacked the one thing they both dreamed of.

The man was afraid it would sour their relationship. He loved his wife no less after all the years, but he worried that his lonely presence would cause his wife to turn from him. So he spent longer and longer out of the house taking meditative walks or chopping wood.

"Oh, how I wish for a child," he would mutter to himself. "A son would be nice, but I think I would most like a daughter to cherish as I cherish my wife."

The woman began to fear that her husband was lost to her. And all because he was so disappointed that she had never borne him a child. She spent her days sitting at the window staring out with unfocused eyes at the trees and mountains.

"Oh, how I wish for a daughter," she would sigh. "I wish for any child, but a daughter would be loveliest."

* * * * *

Snow White

One cruel winter day, an old woman came to the door selling herbs. The man was out at the log pile or walking in the fields, so his wife was at home and alone.

"I don't need any herbs, old lady," she told the visitor, "but you must be cold. Come in and warm yourself by the fire for a while before you go on your way."

"Thank you for your kind thought," the old woman said, "but I will not come in. Your home is far too warm for one such as me. However, let me sell you a few of these bitter herbs because they are, I think, exactly what you need.

"This one, for example, if brewed with ewe's milk, will breathe animation into any object. And this one, we people of the snows call it Iceflower, if soaked in the blood of an honest woman will give the gift of a heart to any who eats it."

Well, the woman didn't really listen, but was kind-hearted and deeming the old lady in need of a few pennies she paid the price and took the herbs.

* * * * *

Over the next days the weather set in hard. The snow fell in great drifts and the ground became a cold bed of clean whiteness.

The man brought the animals close up to the house where they huddled for warmth and let him milk them by hand whenever he liked. So there was goat, and cow, and sheep milk in jugs in the larder, and the woman set to to make yoghurt and winter cheese.

Searching for something to flavour the yoghurt with, the woman came across the herbs she had bought. She added a handful of one of them to the mix, stirred it well, and set it to one side to ferment.

Snow White

The woman then turned her attention to the cheese. More stirring, sieving, and straining. She took up the other bunch of herbs to try it in the cheese. Running her fingers down the stems to strip and crush the leaves, she discovered to her surprise that there were a few sharp thorns hidden away under the shoots. One of these caught in the pad of her index finger and she dripped a few drops of blood into the mix.

"I hope that won't make any difference," she thought as she stacked the cheeses in the store to season.

While she worked, her husband passed the time by making a snowman in the yard outside the kitchen door. He shovelled snow from the path and made a mound almost as high as himself. This he patted and prodded and sculpted until you could make out a head and shoulders, and see arms and legs.

He fetched an old string mop for hair and a straw hat to sit on top. Two pieces of broken bottle did for eyes and glinted in the frosty afternoon light.

What snowman would be complete without a carrot for a nose? But he just couldn't get the mouth right. Whichever piece of bent stick he used, the figure always had a sour expression.

On a whim he fetched one of his wife's aprons, slipped it over the figure's head and tied it around the waist. The effect was completed with a pair of old work boots that poked their toes out from under the hem of the apron.

So realistic was the snowman that when his wife next came out of the kitchen with a tray of jars she gave a yelp of surprise, slipped on the ice, threw her hands in the air and covered the snowman in yoghurt.

* * * * *

Snow White

That evening the couple sat around the fire and their usual silence was disturbed by the wife's grumblings.

"I could have hurt myself falling on the ice like that. Whatever were you thinking of?"

Her husband mumbled his apology again.

"And so many jars broken. And the wasted yoghurt. It's not as though we have food or money to waste."

Her husband sighed his apology again.

"And I shouldn't wonder if that apron is ruined, trailing in the mud."

The man was saved from having to find a new way to say sorry by a soft knocking at the door.

When they drew the bolt and lifted the latch, there, with her green eyes reflecting the firelight, stood a young girl of maybe twelve winters with long flowing hair, a pale complexion, smooth skin, and a rather long nose. She smiled unevenly when they invited her in, and only then did the couple realise she was wearing an apron, a pair of boots too big for her feet, and an old straw hat.

The girl seemed quite at home, as though she had never lived anywhere else. And since she showed no inclination to leave, was content to be fed, and tolerated the couple fussing over her, they let her stay. They clothed her in a more appropriate dress, gave her shoes that were a better fit, and decided to bring her up as their own.

Their new daughter was as pure of complexion as the drifting clouds, and her skin was white as the moon. So they named her Snow White.

* * * * *

Over the days and weeks that followed, the couple tried to introduce the girl to the small ways of their household.

From lighting the stove in the morning, through breaking the ice to bring fresh water in for the animals, all the way to goodnight kisses. But, while she was compliant and always responded to requests that she join in and help with any activity, the child was cold and unloving. This did not bother her parents too much: they had enough love to go around.

This is not to say that Snow White was mean or spiteful. She was guilty of no acts of malice. But she also performed no acts of kindness or generosity.

Indeed, Snow White was just pure selfishness. But since she was also straightforward and lacking in deviousness, this gave her parents no trouble and every opportunity to spoil her. When Snow White took her mother's shawl to wear on her shoulders in the frosty mornings, no one was cross – she gave only pleasure because she looked so pretty. When Snow White ate all of the cakes that had been baked only that morning, her parents were pleased to know she was eating well, and were not upset that there were none for them or for the neighbours who were due to visit later in the day. And if Snow White spent long hours in front of the mirror combing her hair, well that was quite to be expected – was she not the most beautiful daughter anyone had ever had?

As she became more settled, so Snow White became bolder. She wandered the land around the house, sometimes not returning until late at night. When that happened, when the moon was dark, when the wolves that the winter had driven down from the mountains were howling, her parents would sit up by the fire and worry. But when Snow White eventually returned they did not chastise her and she would have shown no remorse if they had.

Snow White

Sometimes in the evening, when the family sat around the stove, the man would go out to check the fences and shut up the chickens and goats. And the woman would tear herself away from the warmth to do the milking. When they got back, shaking the snow from their shoulders, stamping the blood back into their feet, and blowing on numb fingers, they would find Snow White sitting where they had left her, but the stove and indeed the whole house were cold and dark. Then they would have to light the fire anew and wait a long while for a hot drink, for the girl never felt the chill and did not think to keep the fire in.

* * * * *

One day, wandering the buildings of the farm, running her fingers through the wool of the sheep's backs and patting the cow's haunches, Snow White came into the dairy. There she dipped her finger in the different pots and sampled the yoghurts. She tested the different cheeses on the shelves using the little scoop-shaped trowel made for the purpose. And so she left a series of holes that tracked her progress through the store until, after trying the cheese flavoured with pieces of damson, and the cheese washed with apple juice, she came to the cheese into which her mother had mixed the dried and crushed petals of Iceflower.

Although the cheese was still unripe, Snow White found it very much to her taste. She cut scoop after scoop from the round block and gobbled it as fast as she could. Then, when she was full, she carefully washed the trowel, and returned to the house, where she told her parents what she had done and apologised for making such a mess of the stored cheeses.

Snow White

And from now on it was clear that Snow White loved her parents as if she had suddenly grown a heart. She took care to say please and thank you. She gave them small gifts of fir cones she found in the woods or polished stones from the edge of the stream. She always told them where she was going and when she would be back. And she did them small kindnesses such as cleaning out the stove in the morning and fetching fresh water.

The family was happy all winter playing together in the snow and the woods. Sledging. Making snowmen. Tracking animals by the prints they left in the snow. They had snowball fights, and laughed as they ploughed through snowdrifts. They stood at the window at night and looked at the icicles that hung from the eaves and sparkled in the moonlight. They ran through the woods like three children, calling to each other and trying to dislodge the clumps of snow that hung on the branches.

You could never have seen a happier family.

* * * * *

When the spring came, Snow White said to her parents, "It is time. There is always a time when children must leave home and go their own way. You will miss me and sorrow for me, but this is the way of the world. Each must make their own fortune, serve their own purpose, and live according to their mistakes."

The parents wept and begged, but Snow White packed a few things, kissed them goodbye, and strode out into the warm spring sunshine. By the time she reached the end of the path, she was already losing the edge of her shape in their tear-blurred eyes.

By the time she was halfway across the meadow they found that the glare of the sun meant they could not

Snow White

quite make out her form properly. And so their memories became a little fuzzy.

    And before she reached the shade of the trees where the path went through the woods, Snow White had quite melted away.

The Faery Feast

There was once a farmer who farmed the hills above Llanpwlldwrfach and was as mean of spirit as the grey bare hills where his sheep grazed in the driving rain. He would prefer never to sell any of his sheep than to sell just one at a price that was too low.

He never let his wife bake a new loaf until every last slice of the old had been eaten, no matter how stale it had become. And, it need not be said, all that hard bread was eaten without a scrape of butter, because that luxury had to be bought from his neighbour or traded in the village. His wife, whose cunning had grown in step with her disappointment, kept a small tin of mutton fat that she carefully collected when her husband let her roast the carcass of an old ewe that had missed its footing on a crag or had simply decided to die and on which the ravens and worms had not already dined too heavily.

One spring morning when the lambs chased each other in a mad packs of boundless and bounding joy, the farmer was walking his land. He liked to check that his neighbours had not moved any of the boundary walls in the night. He liked to watch for signs of predators that he felt sure must be stealing from his flock. He liked to look down on his old cottage to be sure there was no tell-tale smoke from the chimney that would announce his wife's profligate use of firewood. And, most of all, he liked to count his sheep and lambs and perform detailed calculations of how much they would bring at market.

As the farmer approached the Watching Stone that stands on the ridge overlooking the village, he heard a tinkling of bells like flowers ringing in the breeze. Dropping to a crouch, the farmer watched as a procession of the Fair Folk stepped out from behind the rock, walked under the rowan tree that stood guard there, and set off

The Faery Feast

along the ridge away from where the farmer hid. The farmer quickly covered one eye so that the fairies would not know he was watching them, and gave thanks that the wind blew from the south so that his scent was carried away and did not alert the fey folk of his presence.

Once the troupe had gone from sight and the chiming of their bells was lost in the air, the farmer rose up and decided to investigate. Fairy palaces, he knew, were often said to be full of treasure. Rich pickings would surely await him with the owners far away.

Passing under the boughs of the old rowan tree, the farmer held his breath and stepped briskly into the rock.

He found himself in a great hall lit with a hundred candles and warmed by two great fires, one at each end of the chamber. A long table ran down the length of the room with soft chairs arranged at comfortable intervals. In the middle of one side were two thrones of ancient carved wood with high backs and antlers mounted overhead – clearly where the lady and her lord would expect to sit.

Laid out on the table was a vast feast. There were pies and fresh fruit, cheeses and roasts, steamed vegetables and salads, pâtés and pasties. As he admired the food, the farmer realised just how hungry he was. He had had an early start, had walked many miles, and today had been a stale bread day.

So he walked along the table picking at bits and pieces as he went. A biscuit here, a radish there. Soon his search for riches had turned into an interest in dining.

He pulled out a chair, seated himself at the table, and took a large helping of potato salad. It made him feel more hungry, so he popped a hardboiled egg into his mouth and reached for the pickled onions.

The Faery Feast

Now he was getting into his stride. He cut a large slice of bread, loaded it with roast beef, spooned mustard on top and set about this hearty dish with the silver cutlery at his place.

He grew hungrier as he ate, and reached for a game pie as he still chewed the beef.

And on he ate, and eating was not sated. He ate more yet was never filled. And always craving, still fed himself freely and with increasing desperation until, his lips sore from the passage of food, tears of pain and frustration in his eyes, he shovelled the food ever more furiously to his mouth.

Once he stabbed his tongue with the tines of his fork. Once he caught the roof of his mouth with the splintered bone of a goose leg on which he gnawed. More than once he bit his own cheek in his frenzy. And yet the only sustenance he received from his labours was what he drew from his own blood that he swallowed.

For all I know, he sits there still. Forever eating: chewing and swallowing. Forever desiring, but going unsatisfied. Or perhaps the fairies took pity on him and turned him to ash.

The Caring Father

Imagine a king with unlimited wealth. His cellars crammed with chests of gold coins and gem stones, his table laden with gold and silver plates, and his robing rooms overflowing with silks and furs. Such a king could want for nothing.

Think about a king with complete power. His steward and sheriff standing ready to serve his whim, his soldiers willing to execute his every order, and his pages, cooks, and ladies working all hours to keep him satisfied. Such a king could fear for nothing.

What would you say about a king who had the most beautiful young daughter? The light in his mornings, the joy in his heart, and the blossom in his garden. Unmarried, courted by all, a prize beyond measure. Such a king would live in fear and would be always wanting.

How should such a king behave? Should he lock his princess in a tower to keep her safe from all the young men? Should he pick a handsome husband for her? Would he be wise to find an old duke, rich in his own right, and require her to marry him? How was the king to handle the endless stream of suitors?

After months of thoughtful days and sleepless nights the king knew he had to find a solution. His child would soon be twenty-one years old and if she was still unmarried at that age she would surely remain a spinster all her life, the king's line would end, and likely as not some other king would step in to steal the throne.

So the king made a proclamation – on the night of the next full moon, all who would marry the princess, whether rich or poor, low-born or noble, must present themselves at the castle. Once they were inside, the great doors would be barred. Then the would-be husbands would be given one hour to hide. After that, the king

The Caring Father

would begin to hunt for them. Each that he found would be put to death until just one remained, and that cunning and skilful individual would become the prince and inherit the kingdom.

Now, you might think that the risk would be too high for any to venture this challenge, but you would be mistaken. The reward on offer was beyond anything available by other means: not just the hand of the most beautiful girl that anyone knew, not just acquiring the richest and most powerful monarch as a father-in-law, but, by dint of marriage, to become heir to all that wealth and power. So two hundred and seventy-six came, and at the appointed hour the great hall was full of hopeful adventurers. The door was shut, and guards were posted outside. The king buckled on his sword and set a sand clock to run. Then he sat back to wait as men ran from room to room searching for a hiding place, squabbling and fighting among themselves for the best spots.

At the end of an hour the king rose and shook the timer – he was nothing if not fair. Then, drawing his sword, he started to search.

The first few were easy: they were standing behind the tapestries and drapes in the very hall where the king had sat. He ran them through, making holes and red stains in the precious cloth and not waiting to see their faces.

The next were no harder, really. Still in the same hall they were found behind the benches, under the tables, in the chests, and up the chimney with only their boots hanging down. These last the king handled by simply stoking up the fire.

And so, as the evening progressed, the king roamed his castle, uncovering old men and young boys alike. He flung open closet doors and lifted bedding, he looked on

The Caring Father

top of wardrobes and inside cook pots, he searched behind staircases and under carpets.

It takes a long time to kill two hundred and sixty men, by hand, with a sword.

Two saved the king some trouble. One had stepped out on to a window ledge, and closing the window behind him discovered that there was no window ledge. He lay spread out in the courtyard. Another had gone to hide in the torture chamber in the dungeon. As he swung shut the door of the iron maiden he discovered the ingenious horror of her embrace.

And at about half past three in the morning, the king, who had been counting carefully, was hunting for just fourteen more bodies: thirteen corpses and one son-in-law.

It was getting harder now and he was pretty sure he had checked everywhere.

No fewer than six were found to be lying around in plain sight pretending to be dead among the piles of failed suitors. These the king helped with their acting by giving them that little bit of extra criticism that made their appearance all the more deathlike.

Another four had all had the same idea to hide among the statues in the long gallery. The king found the first one when he sneezed, but so good was the disguise that he was only certain when he had removed the heads of all of the statues: stone and flesh.

The king had a flash of inspiration and roamed the corridors crying, "Come out, come out! You are the last. Show yourself now and become the prince."

With a sigh, a young man dressed just like the king, stepped from a mirror and eased the kinks from his back and stretched his muscles.

The Caring Father

"Only joking," the king told him and cut him neatly in half.

The remaining three really were good at hiding! The king felt some admiration for their cunning and decided that any one would have met his conditions. But according to his own rules he had to find and kill two more.

After his long night, the king paused for a hearty breakfast. He smiled to think how hungry the last three would-be husbands must be by now. He went to freshen up, taking a bath to clean the blood and gore from his body, putting on clean clothes and then paying a visit to the privy where he found the two hundred and seventy-fourth man squatting amidst the filth under his royal bottom.

That would never do! Cunning is admirable, but stinking of shit is not good. The king pointed that out with the point of his sword.

Two to go. One to live and one to die.

The king got a bit frustrated over the next three days. His searches were more desultory and he became fed up with the whole scheme.

At the end of the week, the king pulled the bodies one by one to the windows and threw them out. They were starting to smell. He counted them again carefully as he worked. Still only two hundred and seventy-three, plus the one who had thrown himself out. Still two to be found.

On the evening of the eighth night, as the king was sitting moodily in front of the fire, there was a sudden plop as the two hundred and seventy-fifth suitor hit the floor having fallen from his perch on the ceiling where he was posing as Neptune in the great mural that graced the dome of the great hall.

The Caring Father

The king leapt up in triumph and ran from room to room again calling, "This time it's true! There is just one of you left. You have won. You will marry my daughter." But there was no answer.

The king brought in his whole staff to help search. They turned the whole castle upside down. They tapped walls for secret passages in the stone, and ripped the wooden panelling from the dining room and lifted all of the floorboards. They pulled the books from the shelves in the library, and tore down the ceilings.

But the two hundred and seventy-sixth suitor was too good. His cunning was so great that he simply could not be found.

And so the princess never did get married. When her father, the king, died not long afterwards, she was still a spinster.

Earl Pendrake seized the opportunity, marched in with his army and his family, sent the princess to a nunnery, and declared himself the new king.

The Wise Men of Kulm

The town of Kulm lies on the Western Plain at an important crossroads of the trade routes from Silvakia to Slovethsia. It makes a convenient overnight resting place for travellers and has a host of stores where people can reprovision for their journeys or replace those items that have been worn out, lost, or stolen along the way.

As is the case for such meeting places, Kulm also has a thriving population providing all manner of services from shoeing horses to mending socks, and from baking waybread to selling soap.

As time passed, Kulm also became a centre of trade in its own right. Tinkers on their way from the southern alps to the east coast would meet and exchange wares with pedlars travelling from the wool towns of the west to the factories of the north.

And so warehouses and stores were built, allowing enterprising and wealthy men to buy and sell, stockpile and hoard and become generally more wealthy. At first the buildings sprawled alongside the four great roads of Kulm and then, when all this space was taken, they were set back, creating a whole network of backstreets and alleys. Later, when the town was crowded, the industrious citizens built in the only other spaces available, digging basements and constructing upper stories.

And the old crossroads became a thriving, congested, and crowded town. Here there was affluence aplenty offset by all the poverty and desperation that such centres of commerce attract or create.

In the quieter parts of Kulm the rich merchants built their townhouses with tall hedges and stone walls to keep out the poor labourers who slept in the alleys or

The Wise Men of Kulm

doorways of the warehouses.

* * * * *

Now, you might say that Kulm was the victim of its own success. The street that made up the great crossroads of Kulm had been made up in quieter days. Good quality cobbles on a bed of sand had seemed more than enough for the feet of pilgrims, the horses of messengers, and the occasional trader's cart.

But now the streets saw far more traffic than had ever been imagined. All day long overloaded carts rumbled through town dragged by tired and despondent horses. Three times each day the post coaches would converge on the fountain at the meeting point of the roads to exchange mailbags, luggage, and dusty passengers. And the alleys and roads were always crowded with hawkers and townspeople dashing this way and that, dodging the horses and the vehicles as they went.

Over the years the poor old roads deteriorated. In some places they sank in hollows, in others they rose in ridges. Cobbles came loose and left holes – a problem exacerbated by bored and mischievous children. The resulting potholes would surely have been used by chickens as nests or for dust baths had it not been for the town's hungry cats and the incessant passing of carts.

When it rained the streets turned to rivers. The gutters, blocked with old cobbles and rubbish, overflowed and the remaining cobbles were slick with mud and horse dung. Great puddles formed in the hollows and small ones in the potholes. Incautious travellers got wet boots and feet, or were coated head to toe with dirty

The Wise Men of Kulm

water sprayed up by passing carriages.

* * * * *

Over time, Kulm, which had once built a reputation as a desirable stopover for travellers and must-visit spot for traders, became known as an ugly and dirty town best avoided.

When possible, travellers skirted the town on foot, finding ways through the fields and establishing shortcut paths. Cart drivers looked for entirely different routes bypassing Kulm completely, nervous of the damage to their carts and wares caused by the perilous state of the roads and cautious of the congestion around the fountain that might delay them for hours.

It became obvious that Kulm's glory days were over and that it risked a massive fall in its fortunes. Eventually this fact percolated even as far as the richest townsfolk behind the shutters of their secluded townhouses. They realised that the town's survival was linked with their own and that something must be done.

One day, after much procrastination, the Guild of Rich Men of Kulm took action. They summoned a meeting with the Wise Men of Kulm to ask them for advice on what should be done.

The Wise Men deliberated long and hard. They meditated in silence; they took long walks in the country; they met for discussions over dinner; and they wrote reports. Eventually, when every avenue had been explored and considered, the Wise Men agreed to meet with the Guild to find out what they wanted to talk about.

At the meeting, which all parties agreed should be in the Queen's Arms, the town's best inn, and which took place only after a fine meal had fortified their spirits and

The Wise Men of Kulm

constitutions, the Grand Master of the Guild of Rich Men gave orders that his Third Undersecretary should explain the problem.

"Wise Men, it would be with humility and modest thoughts that we of the Guild would greet you and welcome you to this meeting as equals were it not for the fact that despite your reputed wisdom, your insightful thought, and your shrewd machinations you are yet poor while we are immensely rich. We, like our fathers, have laboured long and hard to turn modest fortunes into great piles, sparing no one's efforts along the way. You, on the other hand, have received your supposed wisdom as a gift, as it were, from nature without lifting a finger."

The Wise Men knew better than to be offended by this formulaic speech. They knew, for example, who was paying for their dinner. They knew as well that they had been summoned for a purpose, and where there is a purpose a contract will surely follow. And where there is a contract there is a fat fee. Such are the benefits of wisdom.

"Nevertheless," continued the Third Undersecretary, "we turn to you at this time for the great benefit of all citizens of Kulm, yourselves included."

And so the Third Undersecretary set out the situation in complete detail, missing no point that all present might already be fully aware of. And, at last, he came to the point. "Therefore, and notwithstanding the aforementioned, or any other previously unmentioned fact or circumstance, the ancient and may I say superior Guild of Rich Men wishes to commission a solution from the Guild of Wise Men to be delivered not later than Shrove Tuesday next."

Well, the Chief Thinker of the Guild of Wise Men knew how to negotiate. He knew that he was in a position

The Wise Men of Kulm

of strength as the sole purveyor of wisdom in Kulm. So, after only a few hours of discussion and just a small number of bottles of port, it was agreed that the solution would in fact not be delivered until Ash Wednesday.

* * * * *

The members of the Guild of Wise Men worked feverishly to come up with a solution. Some sat and thought for a while; others took sedate walks in the afternoon; more still stayed up late at night staring into the fire. In short, they did all of the things that truly wise men do when they have a problem to solve.

They came together from time to time, but never more than twice a day, for sumptuous meals (at the expense of the Guild of Rich Men) and sipped expensive brandy as they cogitated into the night. In short, they spared no expense in their search for the right answer.

But soon it was Ash Wednesday and the Chief Thinker found himself addressing the Guild of Wise Men, a suitable repast having been consumed.

"We have pondered this problem to the full extent of its ponderability and beyond. We have plumbed its depths and measured its girth. We have spoken with travellers dining at the inns of the town, and we have debated with the tradesmen over lunch at the hostelries.

"One thing is clear to us: something must be done. Our town is falling into disrepute and before long our reputation will be ruined. Wagons have been damaged and passengers hurt. Horses have stumbled and their riders have been thrown. Pedestrians have been injured by loads falling from carts, or have twisted their ankles in potholes. In the winter, ladies have slipped on ice and broken bones. In the autumn, babies have drowned in

The Wise Men of Kulm

puddles. In the summer, children have been run down by coaches. In the spring, love-struck couples have been trampled by horses. A solution is needed.

"To fix this problem will cost money. It will need sand and cement, stone and wood, labourers and craftsmen. But if you will fund all of this, we will fix the problem."

The Rich Men were impressed. A solution had been delivered and, although they were not keen to spend their money – and in such large amounts – they recognised that the more something cost the better it inevitably was. So they agreed to all the Wise Men's demands and that work should start at once.

* * * * *

All through the summer whole armies laboured under the instruction of the Wise Men. Wagonloads of stone and timber and sand were brought into the town. The streets rang to the sounds of hammers and saws. Eventually, on All Hallows', the Wise Men sent word that the work was complete.

After another suitably rich and triumphant meal, the Grand Master of the Guild of Rich Men said it was time to see for himself the results of the work and money. So the combined forces of the two guilds staggered out of the Queen's Arms and into the street.

Two Rich Men immediately pitched on to their faces into a large puddle and had to be dragged to safety. Within less than ten paces another had stumbled on a loose cobble and, by the sounds he made, may have broken a leg. And as the group progressed along the road, more and more sustained one injury or another.

The Grand Master, nursing his broken nose, called a halt.

"I bon't umberstabbed," he said. "Pwhad hab you sbett de bunny ob? Pwhad hab you achiebed?"

"Why are you making such a fuss?" asked the Chief Thinker from his position of relative safety on a firm piece of ground at the side of the road. "Can't you see from here the fine building at the end of the street?" And he indicated a lovely stone structure of four storeys with wide windows and green shutters.

"Are you bad?" asked the Grand Master. "Pwhad use is dad to us?"

"Oh sir," sighed the Chief Thinker. "I marvel at your lack of perspicacity. That, sir, is just what the town needs in these terrible times. That, sir, is a hospital."

Seven Swans

A poor girl sat by a lake. She picked stones from the shore and threw them into the water. With each stone she made a wish.

"I wish I had food to eat tonight."

"I wish I had a pot to heat water over a fire so I might have a warm drink before bed."

"I wish I had a blanket to wrap myself in to keep off the chill."

"I wish I had a pillow for my head, not just another rock."

"But most of all, I wish I had some food."

Just then seven enormous swans came by. The largest and whitest swan approached her at the shore.

"We have been cursed," he said. "A cruel witch has transformed me and my companions into the form of birds. We are doomed to remain like this until some honest and fearless person is willing to help."

Well, the girl wasn't quite sure she was honest, but she knew no fear. What is there to fear when you have nothing? So she asked how she could help.

"It will not be easy," the swan told her. "You must spend three nights in the ruined tower between the edge of the lake and the wood. Bad things will happen, but you must not leave the tower between sunset and sunrise if we are to be helped."

The girl had already spotted the ruins and planned to sleep there anyway. It was the only shelter in sight. So she told the bird she would try to help.

On the first night the girl had only just fallen asleep when she was awakened by an old woman shaking her shoulder. The woman was dressed in grey and had a grey face. She started to talk to the girl about her long life, and the girl quickly realised she would not get back to sleep.

Seven Swans

When the moon rose it shone through the walls of the ruin where the stones were missing. It lit up the face of the old woman and the girl could see worms crawling out of her ears and into her nose. And maggots were feasting on her eyes. The flesh hung from her cheeks in rotten strips.

The woman explained that she was dead and had been buried six months ago. She continued to tell the girl the story of her life.

When the sun rose the girl was very tired but the woman disappeared, leaving nothing more than the smell of decay, a few worms wriggling on the flagstones, and the memory of her face.

The swans greeted the girl at the side of the lake. They were pleased to see her and had brought fresh bread and milk which the girl ate gratefully after she had washed in the waters.

After sleeping all day in the sun, the girl entered the tower for the second night. She made up a bed of fern fronds and settled down. But she never managed to fall asleep because she was immediately disturbed by loud shouts and swearing.

Two very rough men were sitting on either side of her, arguing across her body as if she was not there. They were rowing about the best way to kill someone. They described all of the different ways to separate someone from their life. One explained how you could turn a body inside out if you opened their stomach with a knife. The other said it was far more interesting to tie each limb to a different horse and then frighten the animals and see what happened.

"Why don't you take your quarrel somewhere else and let me sleep?" the girl asked them.

Seven Swans

"We don't want to move in case our heads fall off," one replied.

"Don't be so stupid," cried the girl and gave them both a big shove.

But when they were rocked by her pushing, their heads flopped off and hung by their necks. One had his head dangling down his back. The other's head drooped in his armpit.

The men explained that they had been hanged until their necks broke for the crime of burying an old woman alive. Their executioner, they said, had been most professional and had taken particular pains to kill them well.

The girl apologised and helped them set their heads back on their shoulders. They spent the rest of the night competing to tell the girl different ways to skin babies or boil old men.

In the morning the two murderers disappeared and the swans met the girl with more food.

The next night the girl expected to be kept awake again, but nothing happened, and when the clouds covered the moon she managed to doze a little. But she was woken later by a quiet scraping sound. Again and again, as regular as clockwork.

Hunched over a brazier of glowing coals was a huge fat man in a leather apron. He had a leather hood over his head and he was sweating profusely as he sharpened an axe with a stone.

The girl lay still because she did not want to be noticed.

After a long, long time the executioner put his axe on one side muttering, "Shame not to use it. Perhaps later."

Seven Swans

    He then picked up a rope and began to grease it. He was very thorough and the grease was not very fresh-smelling. Then he tied the rope into a noose. He tested the knot several times and hung the rope from a beam.

    "Shame not to use it," he said. "Perhaps later."

    The girl lay even stiller and the man picked up some irons and started to heat them in the fire. From time to time he pulled one or another out of the coals and spat on it to see how hot it was.

    "Shame not to use them," he sighed. "Maybe later." The girl lay completely still.

    In the morning the torturer disappeared and the girl went to find the swans.

    At the lake there were no birds to be seen, but on the pebbles of the beach were seven large tortoises. The biggest of the seven lifted its head and looked at the girl.

    "Thank you," it said. "We were seven tortoises living happily together when the evil witch turned us into swans. Unfortunately she was buried alive before she could reverse the curse. But now we are back in our correct forms.

    "Unfortunately," he continued, "as tortoises we can't bring you any more food because it would take us too long."

    "Don't worry," said the girl. "I have everything I need for a good soup."

    "But where are your ingredients," asked the tortoise, "and how will you carry water to your fire and heat it up?"

    "I hear tortoise shells make excellent cookpots and their meat is very sweet," said the girl.

The Drawing

A peasant sitting outside his hut one day idly picked up a piece of wood that was charred from the cooking fire and started to scratch a drawing on the wall by his side.

He was no artist and he put little effort into his picture. It might have been called a rough sketch had the man given it a little more care or had he had a little more aptitude.

His friend Rudolfo dropped by later in the day to see if he could borrow some chewing tobacco because his own had no flavour left. While the peasant rummaged around in his hut, Rudolfo looked at the black lines scrawled on the wall.

"What's this supposed to be?" he called out. "It looks like something from a nightmare, or maybe that girl you used to fancy from over the mountain. You know, the smith's daughter, the one with the teeth?"

"Are you laughing at me?" the peasant asked. "It's only a rough sketch. But I'll have you know that is a picture of the king."

"The king? Our king? The one in the castle? That's really funny! Doesn't our king have one ear on each side of his head?" And Rudolfo wandered off chuckling and chewing tobacco.

* * * * *

Well, the peasant was a bit miffed. Normally he would have forgotten about his scribbles, and the lashing rains of a few autumn storms would have scrubbed the hut clean. But now he felt he should do something. So he built up the fire, selected and sharpened a few sticks, and carefully baked them in embers.

The Drawing

Then, equipped with his new charcoal, the peasant set to work on his drawing.

He added an ear on the left-hand side, and he took his knife to scuff out one of the ears on the right-hand side. He added a moustache in the latest style, and he made an attempt at a flowing gown.

His friend Rudolfo must have been gossiping because it wasn't long before the neighbours started to drop by. Even though the peasant rarely saw any of them except, perhaps, on hiring day, all of the farmers from round and about found some excuse to call in. Some wanted to discuss the price of turnips, others to ask whether the peasant had seen any bream in the stream, and still more to get an opinion on whether to burn the stubble or plough it in. But of course, they had all come to see the drawing on the side of the hut.

Some of the neighbours managed to disguise their chuckles quite well. They said things like "Well I never," and "Oh my goodness," before turning away thinking, "Fool! What makes him think he can draw? If he gave half as much attention to his roof he might have a dry bed to sleep in." But the peasant could hear their raucous laughter as they walked away down the lane.

Other neighbours cared less for the peasant's feelings, or were much more honest. They criticised his work saying, "Didn't Mother Cavaglli's sow do something like that when it got into church last Candlemas?" and asking, "Is it really supposed to be the king? He (it is a he, isn't it, only it looks a bit like a woman?) doesn't look very regal."

* * * * *

The Drawing

"They're all laughing at me," the peasant muttered to himself, "but I'll show them."

In the usual way of things, the peasant couldn't stick at a task for more than ten minutes before his mind wandered off to think of something else, or nothing at all. So the drawing would have been bleached by the winter sun and forgotten by all except those with spiteful memories. But the peasant had been stirred to an unusual passion and was determined to perfect his work.

Fearing the effects of the weather on the outside wall of his hut, the peasant borrowed a saw from the coffin maker and cut his drawing from the wall and carried it inside.

It must have left a hole at least two ells by three, but the peasant was pleasantly surprised at how it let in the light and enabled him to sit up in bed and work on his picture all afternoon.

The first thing he did was add a crown. That would make sure that everyone knew it was the king.

Then he made the ends of the moustache turn down to look more solemn and kingly. And he did his best to restore a flat chest to the figure.

And he drew the castle in the background so there could be no mistake.

If truth be told, the peasant had never seen the royal castle and never listened when others went into raptures over its grand turrets and fine windows. But he knew the general principle that the king lived in a great house.

Of course, with a large hole in the side of his hut, a bitter wind was soon whipping around the peasant's ears and snow blew in to drift on his blanket. His fingers were too cold for the peasant to grasp his charcoal properly and he became quite miserable, not on account of the

The Drawing

chill gnawing at his bones, but because he couldn't see how he would ever finish his picture.

Then the peasant had a rare and startling inspiration. So unusual was this in fact that it was a full two days before he actually comprehended his idea. But once he understood his plan he put it into action immediately.

He picked up the chunk of wooden shuttering that had, until recently, been an important part of his hut, wrapped it in his blanket and headed for the inn, The King's Fist, in the market town at the end of the valley where the rivers met and where there was a bridge most years unless the spring floods had swept it away again.

* * * * *

Settled in a warm corner in the inn, the peasant uncovered his picture and contemplated his work. He tried to decide what to add next.

Very soon he was receiving helpful comments from some of the regulars who had been in the hostelry for more than a few hours.

Some of the suggestions were a little complicated but seem to involve root vegetables. One comment was particularly perplexing and came direct from the innkeeper's wife: it sounded as if she was offering him a drink while at the same time suggesting he should lay a fire in the grate and visit his mother's grave in some far distant country.

But soon a small crowd had gathered to look at the picture, elbowing each other, pointing out details, and commenting in far from hushed voices. And someone or other stood him a drink, which made the hectoring

The Drawing

innkeeper's wife shut up and go back to mopping tables and picking up broken glass.

The peasant started to pay attention to what was being said. Mainly his admirers thought that his work was drab. It needed colour. Someone had an idea about where the peasant could get a nice shade of brown. Another voice cried out an opinion about where he might source a yellow pigment. But when a pickled beetroot donated by a patron sitting across the room bounced off the peasant's forehead and landed with a slight squish in the middle of the portrait, the peasant realised that adding a rich, royal red was exactly what was needed.

* * * * *

Over the nights that followed the peasant worked carefully with charcoal and beetroot.

Colouring the royal robes was a first priority. And adding some rosy cheeks to convey the health and virility of the kingly figure.

The peasant also added a rose bush as an excuse for more beetroot, a sword because it displayed majesty, and a root vegetable because everyone insisted that it was important.

Then, one evening, it occurred to the peasant that maybe he was only being bought one drink each night, and that of the very poorest ale. People still came to look at his work, but mainly they just snorted or said, "Same as before. Just red and black. Doesn't really make you think of the king with his blue tunic in his green garden with his white horse and his silver lady."

One morning, as he was preparing to return to his hut, the peasant quite distinctly heard three revellers heading home while leaning on each other. Some of the

The Drawing

things they said about the peasant were rather rude, and they laughed uproariously every time one of them mentioned the picture.

The peasant didn't much care what anyone said about him. When you own nothing and have no food, you can't afford pride. But maybe the spring sunshine stirred something in him. He packed up his piece of wall, swaddled it in his blanket, and went back to his hut in the hills.

* * * * *

The matter of colour was a challenge for the peasant. He tried, but rejected, the suggestions he had been given for yellow and brown: they didn't give the right sensory impression. But he found some blue flowers, and green leaves that would serve. He also stole some limewash from the mason that gave a good white.

Silver was a real problem. The peasant took it for granted that the king's lady must truly be coloured silver because that's what they had said. But on reflection, what was silver if not white and black correctly mixed? So the peasant continued his work.

* * * * *

All through the springtime months the peasant worked away. As nature added colour and detail to her great landscape painting of the hills and valleys, the peasant strove to add the right hues to his picture. Nature, rising at first light, added the soft pale emerald of new leaves and delicate washed-out pink of fruit blossoms. The peasant in his wisdom also worked with green, contributing vivid trees and the lawns of the palace

The Drawing

garden. Rising shortly after noon, the peasant worked non-stop every day without a break except for meals and to have brief naps in the sunshine. And he rarely ceased his toils before mid-afternoon.

The king's horse took the peasant quite some days to get right. First there was the challenge of keeping the white white – in the end he considered that a little seepage of green into its head was not crucial. Then there was the issue of getting the legs all the same length, and in the correct corners.

* * * * *

And what did the peasant do for food in these weeks of industry? How did the artist keep body and soul together?

Well, it turned out that his fame had spread and his celebrity brought him visitors. The noblemen of the court diverted their hunting parties so that they could gaze in awe at the peasant's creation.

In return for the opportunity to stare dumbstruck at the picture, the lords tossed the peasant half-chewed ends of sausages and bread rolls that had become squashed and soiled in a misunderstanding of the word saddlebag. In fact, the peasant had never eaten so well.

But it would not be true to say that the peasant was immune to the scorn his visitors displayed. Wealthy as they were, they seemed to think that he couldn't hear them as they talked over or through him. Or maybe it never occurred to them that this "smelly little man with a dirty face and greasy beard" had feelings and thoughts of his own.

So when they said, "Shockingly primitive," and "Lacking in perspective," in their loud, plummy voices, it

The Drawing

was quite clear to the peasant that he was being insulted even if he had no idea what the actual words meant.

And when the gentlemen pointed and guffawed, the peasant knew that they were ridiculing him. But he also knew that his was a work in progress and that they who had never produced such a portrait of their king on fine parchment, let alone on rough timber cut from the walls of a hut, had no grounds to criticise.

So he threw himself into his work and started to colour the king's tunic blue.

* * * * *

It was at about this time that the lords, returning home from their hunts, started to tell their ladies about what they had seen. The idle women gossiped among themselves and were soon arranging summer outings: picnics in the country to which they were driven in buggies and coaches.

Now this represented a change for the peasant because these fine ladies, and especially the younger ones, were quite keen to talk with him. They asked him questions about his work, pointing at bits of the picture to ask what each represented and to query what had been his inspiration.

It may have been at this time, while the peasant was feeling flustered from all the attention, that he accidentally applied some of his blue a little too far up the king's body. Although he quickly scuffed at it and smudged some charcoal in, he didn't quite manage to remove the bluish fuzz around the king's lower jaw.

By and by the ladies asked the peasant about the queen: why wasn't she in the picture? "The queen is always by his side when he is at home at the palace," they

The Drawing

told him. "She is his constant companion; his shadow. And when he is away to visit other kings in battle or at peace, his queen often walks alone in the gardens."

So the peasant added the queen to the picture as best he could having never seen her. "She must be a woman of some importance," he thought. "And always with plenty of food to eat. A woman of substance, in fact." And all this in lime and charcoal to give the effect of silver.

* * * * *

The peasant grew tired of the visits. He was tetchy with the questions, and gave short and grumpy answers. He had never been at his best before his afternoon nap, and was completely unhappy to be woken before lunch by people peering in through the hole in his wall.

So he carried the drawing out of the hut and rested it against a wall in the sunlight for viewing. He thought of writing a brief message for his visitors. Something to explain the picture and to answer the more common questions. Perhaps also a brief introduction to the life of the artist, and a plea for donations. But all that seemed a lot of effort, and it was a problem only complicated by the fact that the peasant couldn't write.

* * * * *

Even a king will eventually notice the amusements and pastimes of his court. At first, hearing the gossiping whispers, and seeing the poorly concealed laughter, this king assumed he was the butt of some joke and arbitrarily executed a few noblemen, sending their wives to a convent and their children to the kitchens. But when the

The Drawing

behaviour continued he thought to ask his chancellor what was going on. And so he learned of the peasant and the picture, and arranged a day's hunting as an excuse to visit this sight.

Arriving at the peasant's hut one glorious afternoon, the king, accompanied by a huge retinue and smiling at the morning's carnage wrought with spear and arrow, and with blood still on his hands from the latest kill, stood in silence in front of the picture, and no one else dared make a sound.

"Tell me, exactly what am I looking at here?" the king asked eventually.

"Well, sir," the peasant began timidly, "it's a piece from the side of my hut."

"Yes. Quite. I can see the hole that is almost the same size and shape. And tell me, my man, what is this that I can see on the piece of the side of your hut?"

"Well, sir," the peasant answered, fearing that perhaps the king might be a little stupid, "you see it is in the nature of being a drawing. Well, to be honest, more of a picture."

"Ah, yes. Absolutely," said the king with infinite patience and quickly forming his own opinion of the peasant's intellect. "I can, indeed, make out some markings that one might assume are a form of drawing.

"And pray tell me, good fellow, what exactly is this a picture of?"

"It is a portrait, sire," the peasant told him. And then, seeing a flicker of irritation in the king's eye, "That is to say, it is a picture of you."

"Of me?" A royal eyebrow ascended a little, and the king leaned forward for a closer view.

"Tell me," he asked after a long, long pause, "how would a person know, supposing they came across this

The Drawing

picture unexplained, that this was, in fact, a picture of me?"

"That is very simple, my lord. Such a person would only have to ask me, just as you did, and I would be sure to tell them."

The king scowled. "Talk me through it. What is that?"

"Why, that, sire, is a rose bush of the like that I am told is so very present in your lordship's gardens. You can see the blossoms here, and here."

"Oh, yes. Now that you point it out to me," the king said, "I can see quite clearly that those marks I took to be random splatters of beetroot juice are, in fact, deliberately placed. Roses, you say?

"Hmmm, and this, this, erm, cow? Why have you placed a cow in my garden?"

"No, no," chuckled the peasant, "not a cow, my liege. Why ever would there be a cow in your rose garden? Surely it would eat all of the roses. No, sire, you would never allow that to happen, I am sure, you being a proper and organised sort of a king. No, that is your faithful steed, the very same one that you rode up on today while I was resting from my labours. That selfsame horse that stands a short way off eating the tops off my turnips."

"I think you will find three things on closer inspection," the king told him. "Firstly, this is my kingdom and everything in it is mine, so, in fact, my horse is eating the tops off my turnips. Second, and you may have to look very closely to determine this, my champion warhorse has actually only got four legs. This is a fact that surprises some to discover when he can gallop so fast and outstrips all of the mounts of all of my most loyal subjects. And thirdly, and this is a point on which I will brook no debate,

The Drawing

my horse is white from head to hoof: there is not a touch of green about him in any light."

"Well, your majesty, you see an artist must ..."

"Enough! Tell me more about what I can see here. What are these figures?"

The peasant wasn't quite sure how to approach this answer. On the one hand he could say that each was a failed attempt to draw the Queen correctly. On the other hand he could say that they were apple trees.

"Majesty," said one of the noblemen stepping forward, "when we visited before he vouchsafed that each was one of your wives. He said you could tell that because they are all in silver and amply proportioned. I think, my lord, that he has neither seen the majestic beauty that is your wife's noble personage, nor mastered the art of painting in silver."

"Did I ask you to speak?" asked the king mildly. "Was I not holding a conversation with one of my more loyal subjects? Perhaps you would prefer to exchange your life for his and live in squalor in a hut with a large hole in its wall. Or perhaps you would like to hold your tongue."

"Now," the king said, turning back to the peasant, "I can see that there is a large ruinous building in the background. This is perhaps the remains of one of my enemies' mansions after I have sacked it. No wait, that cannot be, for here are my own roses growing in front of it. Tell me, then, what building is this?"

"O excellency," whined the peasant, "it is hard for one such as me to comprehend a castle. As you see, I live in this simple hut with less than four walls, and only part of a roof. How then can I picture in my mind or on my drawing such a thing as a fine palace? I have done my best, according to my humble abilities, to show its glory."

The Drawing

"Well, well," sighed the king, "let us pass by that feature and concentrate on what I may, humbly in my turn, call the main feature of this extraordinary drawing: the rendition of my own figure.

"Most surely can I tell it is me because of the gorse bush adorning my head. But also the purple complexion of the face, the two noses, the green (or possibly yellow) moustache, the bushy blue beard merging into the most enormous blue belly, the large snake I am holding, and the brown shoes that smell of what I must have just trodden in."

"Oh, sire," complained the peasant, "you do me an injustice. That is not a snake. It is your great two-handed sword."

"You have drawn an effigy. Some sort of representation that you claim is me. You show many other figures that you say are women. Why would I be surrounded by so many women? You say they are all my wives, but how can that be? Is it your intention to mock me and cause merriment at my expense?"

"Sire," the peasant responded, "it was my intention to make a serious representation of your majesty, Your Majesty. But everyone who has seen my picture has laughed. Perhaps it is not a very good picture, and after all I am only an ignorant peasant, but at least I have made people laugh."

But the king did not laugh.

"I am, of course, a worthy subject for all of my subjects. Each should aspire to render my likeness according to their best abilities. Although you are entirely without talent, it is in your favour that you even attempted this work. But tell me, wretch," he commanded, "which of us is more worthy of attention?

The Drawing

Which of us is noticed and talked about? Which of us is important?"

"Why, of course, you, Your Highness," the peasant replied, confused and fearing a trap.

"And so it seems that when people came to visit, they came to see me, not you. When they spent time looking at your dreadful picture, they gazed on my image, not your physical form. And when they laughed, they laughed at me, not you.

"You have insulted my wife. You have told everyone that I am a Bluebeard. You have made the whole country laugh at me.

"Of these things, the worst is the laughter. I will not tolerate my country, my office, or my person being the subject of ridicule. I am not laughing!

"But I'll tell you how we can recover from this situation. I know what we can do that will restore my good humour. It will make you a celebrated artist. People may laugh at you, but they will laugh with me."

The king had the artist taken to the city, where he was promised a display of his finest work. There the king had the peasant's feet tied to a horse by a long rope and he was dragged round and round the town until he was quite dead. And finally, the king had the peasant's head mounted in a glass case labelled "A Primitive Idiot" and all of the children from the school were brought to see it.

The Tortoise and the Wise Man

There was once a wise man who lived comfortably in a cave at the edge of the desert. He had everything he needed: a soft bed and a warm fire at night, and the glorious sunshine during the day.

For food he made do with the gifts he received from the villagers who trekked out to see him to get his advice. Bread and cakes from the housewives; cheese, tomatoes, and olive oil from the farmers; wine from officials and dignitaries. There was always a trickle of a stream at the back of the cave, but the old man had little use for this element, spurning washing and preferring drinking wine to diluting his bodily fluids with water.

Despite his age, the wise man was surprisingly fit and wiry. Only his bald head shining in the sun gave any clue to the number of years on which his wisdom was based.

One day a tortoise happened by. He stopped outside the cave and he and the wise man fell to discussing philosophy.

"Everything is relative," maintained the tortoise.

"Not so," countered the wise man. "Relatively speaking there are some things that are not everything and those things are ipso facto and de rigueur scrupulously bound to be not related to other things. Besides, I once knew a man who had no children, no brothers or sisters, and no parents."

"Let me give you an example," said the tortoise. "Do you see those tall rocks in the distance?"

"The Pillars of the Ancients?"

"Quite. Yes indeed. I believe that if we were to hold a race, I could get there long before you."

"That has to be worth a bet," sneered the wise man. "But tell me, how do you figure that out?"

The Tortoise and the Wise Man

"It's simple," drawled the tortoise. "I may be slow and steady, but once I start my motion is steady and constant. It is easy to compute my arrival time if you know the distance and my speed. You, on the other hand, are a philosopher, and so you can never get there."

"Now you're just being silly," the wise man laughed. "I'll stake my reputation on it."

"No it's true," the tortoise maintained. "I'll take your bet. You'll lose because, you see, before you can get there you must go halfway there. And before you can go the second halfway there, you must go half of that distance. And so on. You will always have a little way left to go and you will always have to go half that distance first. You can never arrive!"

"We'll see about that" the wise man declared, and set off a once.

The tortoise sighed and, after a pause to consider the perfection of its argument, set off at stately pace in pursuit.

The day was hot. The sun beat down. It was a desert.

A little over three quarters of the way to the pillars the wise man reached an oasis. There were trees and there was shade. The wise man knew he was well ahead of the tortoise: he knew the distance and he knew the speed. So he settled down in the shade for a snooze.

The tortoise plodded on. An eagle high above saw the slight movement and stooped to investigate. Settling on the sand beside the tortoise it asked, "Are you edible?"

"Oh no, not at all," came the muffled response from deep within the shell where the tortoise had withdrawn for safety.

The Tortoise and the Wise Man

"Are you sure?" the eagle asked, pecking at the shell. "You sound edible. Why don't we see if we can't coax you out?"

The eagle seized the tortoise in its mighty talons and with a flap of its great wings took to the air. Riding the thermals the bird rose ever higher.

"This is a terrible mistake," complained the tortoise. "You should know that I can't fly."

"I'm counting on it!" the eagle chuckled.

The day had progressed. The sun had moved around. Or, since everything is relative, maybe it was the shade that had moved. Or perhaps the trees. Anyway, the wise man now dozed in full sunlight.

From way on high the eagle spotted a large and obvious rock in the monotony of desert sand. Just what was needed to crack open this talking lunchbox. With perfect precision the bird hovered and then released its cargo.

Plummeting downwards, the tortoise shared the same impression as the eagle. Certain death awaited it on the ground below.

The wise man never knew what hit him, but he chose that moment to stop being wise. Indeed he stopped being everything.

The eagle swore in disgust and soared away in search of newborn goats.

After a suitable pause, the tortoise stuck its head out of its shell, muttered "I told you so," and set off towards the tall rocks in the distance.

The Boy Who Flew to a Better Place

My grandfather owned a magic carpet. He didn't use it much because, he said, he thought it was a bit showy. But sometimes, if the weather was good, he would take a picnic down to the river and sit there just above the flowing water eating his sandwiches. And, of course, on market days he would use the carpet to save him having to carry his groceries back up the hill to his house.

One of my aunts had a flying trunk. She mainly used it when she went travelling for her holidays, preferring on those long journeys to climb inside, close the lid, and snooze until she reached her destination. But she also liked to stand up in the box when she dotted around the neighbourhood visiting her friends for coffee and cake, or for a hand of whist on a Friday evening. On these occasions she cut quite a figure, waving regally to the people below as she stood braced against the breeze with her hair and scarf streaming out behind her.

This story is about a boy called Bran. It is quite true, just like all my other tales, but I have changed the name of the city where Bran lives so as to protect him from unwanted attention and idle gawpers.

* * * * *

Bran lived in the city of Schmertz on the banks of the great Pošný River.

Schmertz was a city of industry. In every building there was some form of work carried out. In the big factories by the docks, fires burned all day every day and the streets rang with the sounds of hammers on steel, the rasp of saws, and the cries of traders. As in all such cities, the sky was permanently dark with broiling clouds of smoke and steam that settled like drifting snow as a layer

The Boy Who Flew to a Better Place

of black soot over everything and everyone. No plants grew among the grim stone and brick houses that crowded the narrow cobbled streets.

Great fortunes were made in Schmertz. Rich men (and they were always men) traded goods or founded empires of industry making everything from buttons to wheels. And they gave jobs to the swarming masses who flocked to the city in search of wealth and food. Some cleaned the film of grime from the windows of the rich men's houses while others stoked the fires in the hearths or the foundries. Somehow the poor remained poor no matter how hard they worked, and all they collected were sores, and coughs, and wrinkles on their foreheads.

It has never been clear what the relationship is between these things. Maybe ill-health is necessary for dirt and filth to exist. Perhaps poverty is a prerequisite for riches. It could be that riches give rise naturally to sickness.

Into this city Bran was born. And by the time he was ten years old he had a good job. That is to say, he had a job where he was needed as much as any boy who might replace him at a moment's notice and where he was paid almost enough to buy food.

One morning, as Bran set off to work down the street where he lived, he chanced to look up to see whether his baby sister was waving to him from the window in the attic where he lived with his family. He caught a movement against the black clouds of the dawn: something fluttered for a moment and then darted around the corner of the street. Bran ran after it and was just in time to see a shadow dance over the rooftops between the chimneys.

Some said it must have been a bird, but it seemed to Bran totally unlikely that a crow or seagull would have

The Boy Who Flew to a Better Place

risen from the piles of garbage in the streets where they feasted. And anyway, those heavy, angry birds would never dance so lightly on the breeze.

From that morning onwards Bran always kept at least one eye on the sky. On the whole, this was not a wise way to walk around Schmertz: fine if you were perched in the corner of some courtyard or sitting on a window ledge dreaming of supper, but the relentless rumbling of laden carts, the scurrying of men wheeling barrows, and the sparks and splinters flying from open doors meant that you needed your wits about you as you navigated the streets and alleys of the city.

One day, some months later, when Bran was on his way back to his attic room after another long day of work, he thought he caught sight of the shadow in the sky again. This time, not having to hurry to his job, he resolved to chase after the flitting, dancing object.

He followed it across busy streets and down dirty alleys. He chased around corners as it leapt over rooftops. He dodged horses and old ladies, priests and prams, and climbed walls and fences. All in all he was led a merry dance, always no faster than he could run, but never slower.

Then, in a square in front of a church, amongst traders' stalls piled high with all manner of rubbish and between piles of more rubbish on the cobbles, the fleeing thing came closer to the ground. Bran leapt and danced, twisted and jumped, his fingers always just eluded, his feet in all manner of trouble.

Until, tripping over a pail of slops, Bran tumbled and fell and lay panting on his back in a pile of rotting castoffs from the market. His eyes scanned the grey sky for his quarry but he had lost it.

The Boy Who Flew to a Better Place

He sighed and closed his eyes. Almost at once something tickled his nose: a fly or beetle. He brushed it away, but it was back in a moment, insistent.

Several more times Bran batted at it, but each time it came back and tickled at his nose. Changing strategy, he made a grab, and he had it.

Bran opened his eyes and examined what he had caught. A large, crinkly thing that felt like leather between his fingers, it was mottled green and orange and brown. The darker pieces looked fragile, and the whole thing had lines running through it like the veins in his grandmother's leg (or, come to think of it, in his grandfather's nose).

The thing fluttered in his hand as he carried it home, as if it would happily be off on its travels again, so Bran clutched it tightly.

"That is called a leaf," Bran's mother told him. "They grow on trees outside the city where there is less dirt and everything is green. I used to go there once, when everything was a bit easier and we didn't need to work seven days a week."

"I'm going to keep it," announced Bran. "It's pretty." And he placed it on the table under the heavy candlestick so it would not drift away when no one was watching.

Every evening when he got home from work and after carefully checking that the door and window were shut, Bran would lift the candlestick and let the leaf flutter around the room. Some days the leaf would be hard to catch, dodging behind the furniture and staying out of reach. Other times it came to sit on his lap, allowing Bran to softly trace the lines on its surface with his finger.

Then one day there was an accident in the ironworks where Bran's father had a job pouring molten metal into moulds ready for the blacksmiths to work them

The Boy Who Flew to a Better Place

into all manner of useful things. Hot liquid metal splashed from the crucible and the man was turned to steel from the waist down. Realising this, the top half of his body decided not to bother with life any further.

Left with two children to feed and each of them only earning enough for part of what they ate, Bran's mother searched hard for a new husband. This she quickly found in the shape of a brickmaker from another part of the city. He was interested enough in the woman, but would not take in her children, so they were left to fend for themselves as best they could.

Each morning the children rose hungry to go to their jobs. Each day they worked longer and harder. Each evening they crawled into bed with empty stomachs. Bran rarely had time or energy to play with his leaf, and when he did there was no furniture for it to hide behind for it had all been sold.

Late one evening, long after the dark of the day had been replaced by the black of the night, Bran sat stroking the leaf while his sister slept.

"Oh," he sighed, "how I wish I could fly like you. If I could I would surely leave this city and this misery far behind. I would travel to a better place."

The leaf hovered in front of him and Bran reached out to take it by the stem and put it back under its candlestick for the night. But as his fingers closed around the stalk, the leaf floated upwards and Bran's feet left the floor.

He was carried across the room, through the window which he had hastily unfastened, and out into the street.

From above the rooftops Bran looked down at the fires and lamps of the city. And then the leaf lifted him into the clouds and he lost sight of everything he knew.

The Boy Who Flew to a Better Place

Who knows how much later, the boy and his leaf came out of the clouds and the sun was shining. Below them the world was green. They drifted to the ground and Bran found himself standing on grass for the very first time and looking at trees as his mother had once described them.

He explored this new world with his leaf dancing at his shoulder and buzzing around his head. While Bran drank from a clear stream, the leaf did a few pirouettes with a passing butterfly. When Bran picked and ate fresh fruits from the trees, the leaf chattered with its green cousins on the branches.

"What a perfect world," thought Bran. "My little sister would love it here." And birds sat in the trees singing.

A short walk away the trees grew thicker. Bran sat with his back against a trunk in their shade and looked out at the view of gently rolling hills. Some rabbits hopped quietly across the grass in front of him and flowers waved in the sunlight. The leaf held a long dancing conversation with its golden brothers and sisters huddled among the roots or stirred into swirling heaps by gusts of wind.

Bran breathed the clean air, felt the warmth in his bones, and dozed, completely relaxed.

When he woke, a tall blonde girl in a white dress stood by his side regarding him carefully.

"Welcome!" she said. "Do you like it here?"

Bran told her excitedly what he had seen and how beautiful it all was. The girl smiled with joy and, sitting herself beside him, produced a basket of oatcakes and honey and nuts and fruit for them to share.

Later they walked side by side over soft turf and across chalky downs. The girl sometimes stooped to pick a flower for her hair. Bran paused occasionally to examine a nicely shaped stone, or to pick up a pleasing stick. He could not recall having ever been so happy.

"What are you thinking?" asked the girl.

"I am thinking how delightful this all is. I am thinking how I should love to stay here forever."

"That may be easier to arrange than you think," the girl told him. "For you only have to wish it and it will be so. Do you wish it?"

"Oh, I do, I do!" cried Bran.

"Then it is so," said the girl stamping her foot three times on the ground. "And now, what would you like to do next?"

"Why, that is easy," replied Bran. "I should like to fetch my sister. She would be so happy here."

"We will see about that by and by," the girl told him. "But first, you must come and see where I live."

Bran was led along a winding path, down from the top of the hills and into a pleasant bowl-shaped valley that captured the sun. Here, beside a pen that contained two goats, and pecked around by chickens, stood a round wooden hut with a thatched roof.

"Come inside," the girl told him. "I think you'll be pleasantly surprised." And she grinned broadly as she opened the door.

The hut was nothing but a staircase. Broad and clean, illuminated by torches flaming at the walls, the stone stairs led down and into the hillside.

Fifty or maybe one hundred steps (Bran forgot to count) of pale rock finally gave way to a spacious hall lit by large windows with magnificent views of gardens and forests, parks and rivers, cities with gleaming spires, mountains and oceans. Each broad sill topped with crystal glass showed a different world outside. Some windows stood open letting in the sunshine or the breezes of a warm night. Others were closed tightly against the fluttering of huge white snowflakes or the light drops of spring rain.

And there were doors, too. Great big double doors of age-darkened oak with iron hinges. Welcoming doors of pale pine. Tiny, waist-high doors painted bright colours. All manner and shape of door were there.

The girl took Bran to a normal, unassuming door with white paint and a brass handle in the shape of a windblown leaf. Inside was a cosy bedroom. A fire crackled in the grate, and a blue patchwork cover lay on the bed below a crisp white pillow. Bran tumbled into bed and slept deep for all those long hard hours of his childhood.

Over the days that followed, Bran and the girl went on many adventures. After breakfast, the girl would look thoughtfully around the hall before making her decision. Then they would step through one of the doors and enter a new place. Sometimes she would make Bran change his clothes before they set out: perhaps furs for a trip into the frozen forest, maybe flowing robes to visit the desert tribes. And after every adventure they returned to the hall through some passage or doorway and climbed down the stone staircase to return to their beds.

Every few days Bran would mention his sister because he worried about her alone at home in the dirty alleys of Schmertz. And, to be honest, he missed her as well. But when he asked the girl whether his sister might not come and share the fun, her face clouded over and there was a sharpness to her eyes.

"We'll see about that by and by," was her only answer, and Bran sensed there was no point in pushing the point further.

The Boy Who Flew to a Better Place

As Bran became more familiar with his surroundings he took to wandering from window to window gazing out at the fabulous vistas. He found that he could spend many hours just watching a new scene, and would become absorbed in the patterns of life. Often the girl would come and sit by his side and together they would share the wondrous views.

During these days drifting from one casement to another, Bran noticed that there was one window that was shuttered and one door that was barred. At first he kept this observation to himself, but eventually his curiosity overcame him and he asked his friend, "What lies beyond that window? Why is it so tightly closed? Where does that door lead and why do you keep it locked so securely?"

At once the girl's face grew stern and her eyes flashed with barely suppressed anger. "This is my home, my Hall of Many Places. I will keep locked those doors I do not choose to open, and block out those views I do not wish to see."

But soon her smile returned. "Don't we have a great time together? Can't we travel to every place that exists and many that don't?

"There are some places, however, that are too horrid, too grim, and to which I never want you to go," she told him.

And the next time Bran mentioned his sister, the girl simply glared at him.

* * * * *

One day, rising early, Bran went to the boarded-up window and set to work on it. He pulled open rusted bolts and prised nailed battens from across the opening before finally wrenching open the shutters and looking out.

The panes were darkened with grime and grease, but he strained his eyes. Was that a cathedral? Could that be a town hall? Were those factories with great chimneys belching steam and fumes? Was it possible? Yes, those were the rooftops, those were the alleyways, that was the heaving, dirty mess of a city called Schmertz.

Bran rushed to the bolted door. His fingers clawed desperately at the locks and bars. He shook the great handle in frustration, but nothing would move. The door stayed closed and his way back to Schmertz was blocked.

Back at the window, Bran peered out at his home far below. The view through the dirty window became even less clear as his eyes filled with tears. He struggled with catches and flung the window open so he could smell the familiar stench of Schmertz.

"Oh, how I wish I could fly," he sighed. "If I could, I would surely leave this place of wonders far behind, and return to what I know and what I love."

And there bobbing in front of him, tossed on the wind and just out of reach, was the leaf. Bran climbed to sit on the window ledge, his heels banging on the grey stone wall that stretched downwards for ever, his one hand clutching the window frame, his other stretching out into the void searching for the leaf that was just too far away.

"What are you doing?" the girl's voice came to him, cold and quiet with fury. "Did I not say that there were some places I never wanted you to go? Come back inside immediately."

But as she moved to grab him and pull him back to safety, Bran made another snatch at the leaf, lost his balance and he was falling. His fingers clutched futilely at the air and he kept falling. The wind rushed past his ears as he fell.

Then, suddenly, his flailing hand came into contact with the leaf. He held it firmly by the stalk and it lifted him up again, past the stones of the grey wall, past the open window where a girl in white stood with her blonde hair blowing in the wind, and up into the clouds.

"Where are you going?" she cried after him. "Didn't I grant your wish to stay with me? Didn't I give you everything you wanted? Didn't we have fun together?"

But "Alone" was the only word he heard from the girl's mouth as the leaf bore him away into the soot and smog and noise of his home town. "Alone, alone," seemed to echo through the streets mingling with the sounds of carts, the ringing of hammers, and the curses of porters and labourers.

* * * * *

Bran still lives in the attic room in Schmertz with his sister. At the window, which is always left open to guarantee a draught and a view of the swirling grey clouds, stands a large cage carefully woven from fine wire. In the cage rustles and flutters a single leaf, lifting to dance on a gust of air, or settling gracefully on a perch or on the bottom of the cage as the city moves from busy, hectic day to noisy, bustling night.

The Thieving Magpie

There was once a magpie who lived in a sunny wood surrounded by many other birds.

The magpie, whose name was Clarence, was a shy but cunning creature. Although he felt bad that his feathers were not as bright and cheerful as those of his neighbours, he kept his black and white plumage in perfect order, so that his white breast sparkled brightly when it caught the rays of sunlight and the black feathers of his back and tail were midnight dark and oiled with a sheen that made them almost blue.

Clarence also felt bad that the other birds had fine and bright songs that echoed through the trees all day and at no time more than at first light when all the winged creatures opened their hearts to give thanks for the new day. But he never held back, and would proudly cry out in his harsh and clamouring voice, "Look at me! I'm here too. See how fine I am!"

All through the year, Clarence worked hard to overcome his shyness and ingratiate himself with the other birds. He would perch at the very top of one of the fir trees and announce his presence. And he would hop across the forest clearing in his peculiar two-legged bounce. And all the time he would cosy up to his fellow birds, dropping a few words here and there to pass the time of day.

Before long, the tits and finches would chirp back at him. Even the blackbirds and thrushes exchanged the odd comment.

It was true that the other birds didn't really feel at ease with Clarence: he was larger than most of them, and his shyness and raucous voice were not conducive to long conversations. But they were flattered by his attentions and thought him perfectly turned out in his sombre and

The Thieving Magpie

formal black and white. They were honoured to spend time in his company.

Not long afterwards, some of the birds offered invitations to Clarence to drop by their nests for an evening worm and to exchange a few words on the state of the ornithological world. They did their best to tidy their homes, throwing out the old bits of moss and making a decorative display of pleasing stones and pieces of foil or plastic wrappers that the wind had blown into the wood.

Clarence would hold forth in his strange voice for a while, giving his hosts the benefit of his opinions, and the birds would flock round to hear what he had to say on a wide range of subjects. Encouraged by the attention, Clarence overcame his shyness still further and became an expert on a number of topics about which he had previously known nothing.

And if, after a night explaining how things worked, some small and insignificant sparkly thing found its way under his wing as he was leaving and thence back to his own nest, Clarence considered it only reasonable recompense. Besides, the smaller birds obviously did not understand how to make the most of these baubles: a more discerning eye was needed to bring out the best in these treasures.

If the other birds noticed that Clarence was making free with their possessions they did not say. But some did miss what they had previously cared for, and some lamented the absence of the loved things that had brought hope and meaning to their lives.

* * * * *

The Thieving Magpie

Nuthatches are wild spirits who eschew the constraints of refined society. They build elaborate nests of bark and straw, and in their contrary way they defy all proper behaviour by walking up and down trees as though they were out for a summer's afternoon jaunt among the worm-rich roots of the ash and birch.

One day, a nuthatch happened to be strolling down the trunk of the pine in which Clarence lived. Looking up, or rather down, he saw right into Clarence's nest and was astonished to see it glittering and sparkling with all manner of shiny things. Hopping closer he was suddenly aware of a shadow that closed in on him. And there was Clarence screaming and screaming, "This is my nest! This is my tree!"

"Oh dear," twittered the nuthatch in confusion. "I meant no harm. I was just looking for woodlice. But tell me, isn't that the goldfinch's prized piece of blue glass that I can see there in your nest? And that, isn't that the red feather from old Tom Robin's breast that his widow was keeping to remind her of better days?"

"Mine! All mine," screamed Clarence. "Each one is mine. All found by me. All collected by me. All carried back to my nest by me. All curated by me. No one else could present them as I do. They are all mine and none shall deny it."

"Well, I only asked," said the nuthatch politely. "It's only that it seemed to me ... "

Clarence cut him off with a cry that might have been a squawk. "I will not have anyone in this wood who casts aspersions. I will not have my rightful possession challenged." And he flew at the poor little nuthatch with his wings wide and his fierce beak open. And he harried the honest bird from tree to tree and right out of the wood.

The Thieving Magpie

"And don't come back," Clarence screamed after the fleeing nuthatch. "Find another place to rear your chicks if you can, but no wood will be as good as this one, no trees as full of food, no companions as pleasant as they were here. I expect you will have a hard time, but you brought it on yourself."

When the other birds asked what had become of the nuthatch, no one knew. But Clarence said, "I chatted with him about his future and he decided he was going to try his luck in the meadows down by the river. I tried to talk him out of it because it is hardly the right environment for his type of bird, but he was determined to explore other opportunities. He said that at his time of life it was now or never."

* * * * *

A short time after this, a woodpecker was exploring rotten branches near Clarence's nest and realising, where he was, thought he should drop by to pay his respects and also see whether there were any tasty bugs to be found in the trunk of Clarence's tree.

No sooner had the woodpecker settled on a branch near the nest than Clarence himself came swooping and sailing in to land on top of his nest with wings outspread.

"Oh," said the woodpecker, "that looks most uncomfortable. What have you got in there? It's too early for eggs. Have you made a mistake in the way you built your nest? Move over and let me have a look, perhaps I can help."

Now Clarence was in a tricky spot. He wanted to shout and scream at the woodpecker. He wanted to drive him out of the wood as he had done the nuthatch. But the fact was that the woodpecker was a good deal larger than

The Thieving Magpie

him, possessed of a fearful beak, and rumoured to be rather clever as well.

"No, no," he said, "I couldn't put you to any trouble. It's my nest and I will have to sort it out. Don't you worry."

"Well, look," said the woodpecker kindly, "I think I see the problem. There, sticking out from under your left wing, isn't that the bottle top that the old thrush used to break her snails on? You know, the one she mislaid last winter?"

"No, no," cried the magpie shuffling around on his nest to cover the silver disc with his tail. "You must be mistaken. It's all mine. Definitely. Yes. All mine!"

"But wait," said the woodpecker. "I'm pretty sure that when you were wriggling just then I caught sight of a pebble that looked remarkably like the one I had in my nest in the old holly tree. It was like a small white egg with a black line running through it. My chicks loved to play Mummies and Daddies sitting on it, but I mislaid it sometime last year."

"You must be mistaken," was Clarence's reply, screaming now. In his agitation he found it almost impossible not to flap his wings, but he kept them spread out as much as he could to guard his trove. "It's all mine! My nest. Mine. I don't need any help. It's got nothing special in it. It's just got a few teething problems. I built it. My design. Go away!

"Please," he added, remembering to try not to offend a bird that might make life difficult for him.

"Hey-ho," said the woodpecker. "It's nothing to me if your nest falls apart. And I am not bothered if you have an uncomfortable bed. I'll pop back in the morning to see whether you have changed your mind about my offer of help, and also to see whether you have remembered my pebble." And he flew off in search of grubs for dinner. Before long the drumming of his beak against a dead oak branch could be heard across the whole wood.

Now Clarence was really worried. True, his nest was uncomfortably crammed with stolen things. True, he had no hope of a good night's sleep and had to spend most of each day trying to shore up the sides of the nest against the weight of his treasures. True, he spent a lot of time distracting other birds so that they wouldn't drop by. But he could not risk the woodpecker returning and seeing his special pebble inside the nest. And he would not let the interfering bird help him with the nest because he knew that if the roles were reversed he would demand payment, and there was no way that the magpie would part with any of his treasures.

So Clarence made a trip to see the buzzard, the undisputed ruler of the forest. He put his case quite simply.

"I have become well known in the wood as an impressive figure. Other birds look up to me, and I give this wood of ours a good name. But the woodpecker has become disruptive with his loud hammering at all hours of the day. He is pushy and often insists that his ideas are superior. Why, only today he tried to tell me that my nest is not built correctly. Frankly, he doesn't fit in in this wood any more. He belongs to another time when this was a very different wood. I don't think his presence is conducive to the peace and harmony that are the very essence of your vision for our little patch of trees.

"Ah, I see," said the buzzard. "Perhaps I should let him go."

"Yes, that might be for the best," agreed Clarence. "We will all miss him, of course. He had become part of the furniture. But that is the point, isn't it? We're a forward-looking wood and must move with the times. His departure would be good for the wood and create openings for the other birds. And you will be doing the woodpecker a favour by helping him spread his wings."

"All right, consider it done," said the buzzard. And that very day he visited the woodpecker and explained how, for the good of all the other birds, for the good of the wood, and most of all for the woodpecker's own good, the woodpecker should remove himself from the wood immediately and not come back since he was no longer needed or welcome.

* * * * *

Nesting time came again in the wood. All of the small birds darted here and there from dawn to dusk preparing to launch the products of their labours into the world. Cosseting eggs and nurturing chicks towards their first attempts at flight.

Clarence, who sat alone atop his collection of shiny things acquired by theft and cunning, had no eggs of his own to worry over. Indeed, had he had eggs, he would have had nowhere to put them, so full was his nest of borrowed belongings.

But Clarence kindly offered his help to hard-pressed mothers in the trees around. It was no trouble, he said, for him to take a turn incubating their eggs or babysitting the fledglings while the poor tired ladies got a little rest or hunted for food.

And if, when the mothers returned, there was one fewer egg in the clutch, or one chick had gone missing, no one seemed to notice or care in the flurry of activity. And Clarence was careful not to belch until he was far away and on top of his own nest.

The Thieving Magpie

Sometimes, a mother might tilt her head to one side as if to say, "I could have sworn there were five of them. Isn't little Timmy missing?" and Clarence would tell the tale of how he had tried, tried so very hard, to stop him, but Timmy had been certain that he could fly.

"Oh, I pleaded with him," Clarence would say. "I told him it was too soon. I said he needed to do more exercises, to test his wings better. But he was determined to launch."

And if, sometimes, the nest was half-empty when the parent birds returned, then it was, of course, rather noticeable. At these times, Clarence, wiping the yolk from his beak, would have to make up some story or other to explain what had happened.

A raid by a squirrel or a rook was usually a good cover. He could embellish the tale with reports of his own heroism and how, had it not been for him, the nest would now stand completely empty.

Once Clarence even used the cuckoo as an excuse, saying that he had discovered that three of the chicks in the blackbird's nest were in fact interlopers. He had, as is only right in the circumstances, simply pushed them out.

But gradually, the other birds grew wary. They noticed how raids by squirrels only ever took place when Clarence was there to defend the nest.

In the end, no one liked or trusted Clarence. A few might follow him around, listening to what he said and trying to catch the titbits that fell from his beak as he ate. But none chose to spend time in his company.

* * * * *

The Thieving Magpie

Clarence is still a lonesome bird. Not now because of his shyness, but because all the other birds have worked out who he really is.

He still keeps his plumage immaculate, but his sombre colours don't instil admiration and the stark contrast between his white breast and his black back and tail only serve as a warning of the difference between his first impression and his real personality.

He still sits on top of his pile of shiny things and pecks them over in the sunlight. But there is no one else to admire them and, truth be told, they bore him now.

When he joins in the dawn chorus now, his raucous cry is of despair and loneliness.

Mr Christy and Clever Simon

When witches live in cottages deep in the woods we know what to expect. They trap and eat children. They fly on broomsticks or travel around, somewhat improbably, in a mortar using a giant pestle to steer with and human skulls as fuel.

And we know that so long as we stay out of the dark wood, remain on the path, don't follow the voices, never believe wild animals, and above all don't nibble people's houses, we will be quite safe. And anyway, aren't there certain and foolproof tests involving bells, and candles, and pins, and chairs plunged into rivers, and red-hot irons, and men in black hats?

What if witches don't all have warts on their chins, hair on their upper lips, hooked noses, hunched backs, and crooked fingers? What if witches look just like us? What if they live among us?

* * * * *

Simon seemed to most people to be an ordinary boy. That is, he annoyed his father, upset his mother, frustrated his teacher, and tormented his younger brother without compassion but with a degree of something approaching love.

When he was needed by his mother to help with the chores he could never be found. Perhaps he was hiding in the long grass trying to catch a rabbit, or down by the pond skimming stones. When his father wanted assistance with the fire in the forge, Simon would be found to be absent. Was he up a tree or just in his room with his nose in a book?

And Simon got on well with the people of the village. Unlike with his parents, Simon was always willing

Mr Christy and Clever Simon

to stop and chat, to offer a helping hand, to pass the time of day.

To one side of his house lived Mr Christy, a quiet, tidy, one might even say fastidious man. He was what people used to call "of independent means" which really just said that he always had enough money to get by, but never quite enough to buy new clothes or have lavish habits. But he was always clean and smart, always up early in the morning, and punctilious in his politeness.

In the house on the other side lived a young girl of "questionable virtue". Simon did not have any evidence to doubt her virtue, and she was always very kind to him. But Agnes, as she was known, seemed to work hard, long hours, always taking in mending or washing at any time of night from all manner of visitors.

In the little cottage that sat behind Simon's house lived Mother Wardle. No one knew why she was called Mother because there were no children visible and, indeed, if it wasn't for the kindness of the village folk and her persistent scavenging for edible fungus, Mother Wardle would surely have starved.

Most days Simon would spend at least a little time with one or other of his neighbours. He might chat a while with Mr Christy as he leant on his garden gate, or go into the garden to load a wheelbarrow with the weeds that Mr Christy had pulled up from around his vegetable and herb beds and then transport them to one of the sweet-smelling compost heaps beyond the apple trees. Or he might carry a parcel of slightly stale leftovers from the baker to Mother Wardle and listen patiently while the old lady told him tales he didn't quite understand, put up with her persistent stroking of his hair, politely decline her offers to go into her house which smelled of her, only more so, and discreetly wipe the spittle from his face

Mr Christy and Clever Simon

when she grew too excited. And he might spend an hour or two with Agnes helping her hang up or bring in washing from the lines that criss-crossed her garden or sitting at her feet while she mended socks and pinafores and told strange tales of faraway peoples and peculiar places.

Whatever the people of the village might say, Simon found his neighbours to be nice, ordinary, but interesting folk. He never had cause to fear them, and enjoyed spending time in their company. If the villagers warned against "going with strange people" or of the dangers of "making friends with peculiar adults", Simon had no fear – weren't all grown-ups a little bit peculiar?

* * * * *

It was when Simon was ten that The Troubles started. The adults didn't like to discuss it in front of the young ones, but children are more shrewd than they are given credit for, and walls are thinner than old ears believe. What started as a few naughty children running away from home, and developed into a number of wilful youngsters deciding to seek their fortune in the wide world away from the claustrophobia of the village, quickly turned into an epidemic of presumed drownings, kidnappings by passing tinkers, and starvations while lost in the woods.

Parents who were previously happy to let their children run free and happy now became protective and wary. All of their offspring were required to come straight home from school: no dawdling, no football in the street, no unplanned visits to each other's houses.

There was even talk of a witch, although this was whispered so quietly that only the most artful listeners

Mr Christy and Clever Simon

picked it up and relayed it to the other children.

* * * * *

Simon's neighbours rallied to the crisis in their own ways as best they could. Mother Wardle chuckled a good deal and told tales of the witches of long ago, summoning up images of horrendous hags screeching through the skies on broomsticks in ways that seemed improbable and laughable in the daylight, but a little more sinister if you recalled them in the dark in your bedroom. Agnes clucked a bit and pulled Simon to her more than ample bosom and told him not to worry, and said that any time he was frightened he was to run straight round to her house. And Mr Christy stood at his gate, pipe clenched in his teeth, and watched the world – their own sentinel against uncertain times.

And in these difficult days, Simon may have shown a little more respect for his parents. This is not to say that he was more helpful in his father's workshop or around the house, but he was careful to avoid a scolding by always letting his mother and father know with which of the neighbours he was spending time.

* * * * *

And then there was a period of six weeks in which no child went missing. The tension was almost a physical creature walking the lanes and alleys of the village. The parents with surviving children did not dare to believe that The Troubles were over, but with each day they struggled increasingly to control their offspring. It was like waiting for the proverbial boot to fall on to the floorboards of the lodger's room above your own

Mr Christy and Clever Simon

sleeping chamber. It was like waiting for the thunder after the lightning. It was the certainty of the unconfirmed inevitable. Which child would be next?

Simon, who was more sensitive than his parents might have credited, chose to spend less and less time with Mother Wardle. If the baker pressed a bag of stale buns on him he would deliver them, but not hang around to hear how Goodie Bellane had met her end in the witchfinder's flames, or how Granny Coltstaple had screamed when the silver touched her skin.

But the less time he spent with her, the more interested in him Mother Wardle seemed to be. She crooned and begged and dribbled, and she reached out her gnarled hands with their liver spots and crooked fingers and dirty nails.

"Come let me stroke your hair like I used to," she begged. "Come into my cottage and you'll be completely safe for ever."

But Simon always dodged away and, preferring not to pass through her portal, festooned as it was with the bodies of dried frogs hung on tatty pieces of string, he would scurry home.

Simon also found Agnes more oppressive. These days she seemed to smell more strongly of lavender and rosewater. And she always had a fire smouldering in the garden on to which she tossed sprigs of thyme and wormwood and fleabane.

When Agnes asked for help collecting the washing, Simon still stood with his arms out until he had been loaded up with gentlemen's nether garments and ladies' chemises, but if Agnes asked him to carry them into the house and pile them in front of the fire, telling him he would be quite safe, Simon would politely set the clean

Mr Christy and Clever Simon

clothes down on the stone step by the front door and skip home to his parents.

Only Mr Christy offered a pillar of stability. Each day he stood by his gate, chewed the stem of his pipe, and watched the world. He made no demands on Simon and, when it started to get dark, always sent Simon home to his family.

From time to time Mr Christy would muse about the missing children and the possible causes.

"You see, young Simon," he would say, "I have made a careful study. It is wonderful to see what knowledge you can accumulate if you only sit and watch.

"Of course, I'm only an amateur sleuth. Maybe a bit of a scientist: you know what that means, Simon? I'm not a professional puzzle solver and definitely not a witchfinder. But still, I stand here at my gate and I watch the world and I talk to people and I gather information. And bit by bit I think I see patterns emerging."

Sometimes Mr Christy would talk about the many pages of information he had compiled. But just as often he would tell Simon that he was a foolish man to waste his time this way and order Simon to forget all about it.

Then, one rainy afternoon, Mr Christy told Simon about the map.

"You see," he said, "we build up false impressions of what has happened based on which events resonate with us. Little Robbie Twopennies disappeared down by the wishing stone and since that is a special place for all of us – for who hasn't had a memorable summer picnic with their friends and family at the wishing stone? – we start to believe that this is important. And so we ignore the fact that Harry Gobber, Peter Flem, and Marcie Salver all vanished down by the ford. You see my point?"

Mr Christy and Clever Simon

And Simon did see the issue at once. How could anyone know what was really happening if no one took a proper view of the whole thing?

"So," said Mr Christy, "I have a large map pinned to my wall, and I have stuck in a flag to show where each child that was taken was last seen. I must confess that as yet I see no pattern, but I am hopeful that given time I will work something out."

Naturally Simon asked to see the map for himself, but Mr Christy said that today would not be convenient and suggested that Simon run along home, which he did a little reluctantly, waving at Agnes where she stood in her garden pegging out washing in the drizzle.

So the next time Simon saw Mr Christy at his gate, of course he asked about the investigation.

"I have made several copies of the map and drawn lines between the locations to see whether there is a mystic message," Mr Christy told him. "But I am sad to say all I see is a mess of lines."

And Mr Christy delivered himself of a long and rather sad sigh. "Perhaps I am just a silly man with too much time on my hands. Perhaps if I had a job and had to work for a living instead of fiddling around with maps ..."

And though Simon begged and pleaded, and even when he said he was really good with puzzles and maps, Mr Christy said no. "It's both morbid and pointless. Nip along home to your family and don't fill your head with my nonsense."

So Simon did just that, waving at Mother Wardle where she stood in front of her cottage stroking her black cat that always looked so fierce.

But the next day, a sunny one, Mr Christy opened his gate as Simon walked home from school and said

Mr Christy and Clever Simon

excitedly, "I think I have made a breakthrough. Would you like to see?"

Simon was delighted and gladly let Mr Christy usher him through the garden and into his house.

"Come," he said, "the maps are in my study. Let's go through."

Mr Christy closed the front door and led the way through his house. There was a long corridor that was dimly lit now that the bright sunshine had been shut out. The bare floorboards creaked seemingly independently of the passage of their feet as they passed closed doors. The panelled walls were hung with charts and maps of faraway lands only half visible in the gloom. The faces of ladies and children long dead peered out from dusty frames.

Mr Christy ushered Simon through a doorway and into a cosy parlour. A bright fire burned in the grate. A large sofa stood in front of the window dotted with soft cushions embroidered with animals just asking to be stroked. A golden retriever warming itself at the hearth opened one eye and flicked its tail once or twice in acknowledgement. On the table stood a bowl of fruit and a plate of sugar biscuits.

"Through here," said Mr Christy and led the way around a bookcase beside an upright piano, and Simon found himself in a tiny study. The walls were lined with books and a large oak desk stood filling most of the room. A picture window gave a fine view out over parkland where a herd of deer were strolling and grazing on lush grass.

Mr Christy pulled a tube of paper from a shelf and unrolled it on the desk, moving a lampstand shaped like a ballerina, an inkwell made of blue glass, a badger skull, and a photo frame to hold the corners down.

Mr Christy and Clever Simon

"Here," he said, "is a map showing the last sightings of all the missing children marked with blue stars. You can see that they are dotted all around."

"And what are the red dots?" asked Simon.

"Those are the children's houses. See, there is the McNallys' house where Irene lived."

"Yes, I see," said Simon excitedly. "I know how to read a map. That's Main Street, and that's the butcher's shop where Thomas Weisswurst lived with his father. And that dot must be where Molly Minger and her mother lived behind the tannery – Molly was the first to go missing and her mother left to find a new home far away from her memories.

"So this must be Agnes's house, and here is where Mother Wardle lives. This is your cottage where we are now. But wait! Why is there a red dot on my house? No one has gone missing from there!"

"Ah yes," sighed Mr Christy, "that was a mistake. I got a bit carried away. Forget about that one for now."

Mr Christy waved his hands expansively and explained all the theories he had tried. He used a ruler to explain the patterns that showed up when you joined the blue stars, the red dots, the school, the church, and the bridge. But, as he had described before, no hidden pentagram was exposed.

"What do you think?" he asked Simon. "You're a smart lad. Can you see anything?"

"It seems to me that when you can't find a pattern it is probably because there is no pattern to be found."

"That is very astute of you, Simon. You are quite clever. That is the conclusion I came to. It's reassuring to know there is nothing here that points back at the culprit.

Mr Christy and Clever Simon

"So when I decided that, I started to look at other information." He pulled out a ledger and opened it where it was marked by a crimson ribbon.

"Here is a list of all of the missing children. Next to each name I have noted all of the relevant data: their ages in days; their heights; the time of day when they were last seen; the number of days between disappearances. But I could not see any logic, no way to predict the next child. What do you think?"

"I agree," said Simon thoughtfully. "Whoever or whatever is doing this is most careful to leave no trail."

"It's a relief to have that confirmed," sighed Mr Christy. "You can never be too careful," he wrinkled his brow and added, "in how you analyse the facts."

Simon stared out of the window in silence for a while. An idea was nagging at a corner of his mind.

"Can I look at the map again?" he asked. "Yes," he said, "there is exactly no pattern. It's as though leaving no clues was an actual objective. I wonder whether the absence of a pattern is a pattern in itself."

"Well," said Mr Christy, "perhaps you had better be on your way." And he almost drove Simon out of the study, through the parlour with its bowl of fruit, its plate of biscuit crumbs, and the sleeping dog, down the corridor where the panels creaked and sighed and the children in the pictures mouthed silent words, and back into the daylight of the garden.

Simon walked the short distance home. There was Agnes sitting cross-legged in her garden chanting to herself. And there was Mother Wardle at her doorway holding up a crude doll she had made from straw and beckoning to Simon. He was glad to get back home to safety.

Mr Christy and Clever Simon

That night was warm but dark. The moon was covered by thick, dark clouds. The heat promised a storm and the bedroom windows stood open in the houses and cottages of the town as people tried to sleep.

A flutter at the sill of Simon's room could have been the curtain or a night bird. It was followed by stillness and silence.

Then a sudden crash and a mild oath. Simon lit a candle and studied Mr Christy where he lay face down on the floor, his feet neatly caught in a loop of rope and the grandfather clock resting across his back.

"The thing is," said Clever Simon, "that my red dot was necessary to hide the pattern. If you took it out, and maybe the last three or four others, it was quite clear. So I see why you added it.

"But look at my map on the wall. Oh, I don't suppose you can see it from that position.

"Well, I drew lines from all the windows of your house to the bedroom window of each missing child. And guess what? Each one is a straight line."

"Mumph, frrh, gzrd," said Mr Christy, his face in the bedside rug.

"You might well say that," commented Clever Simon, "but to me it was obvious. And then I realised that while I often saw you in your garden, you never go beyond your gate. And I asked myself why that was.

"Well, on reflection it is obvious. You are a spider. You visit children's beds at night and attach them to a thread. Later, when you're ready, you simply reel them in and trap them in one of the pictures in your hallway until they're ready to eat.

"But it is time for your games to stop," said Clever Simon. And he scooped up Mr Christy's body in an old jam

Mr Christy and Clever Simon

jar, screwed on the lid, and set it on the mantelpiece with the others.

The Donkey with Golden Shit

It was when he was a young boy that Calvin Di Allegori first heard the story of the donkey that shitted gold pieces. The tale, a bedtime staple for all children in the villages of his part of Italy, was repeated by his parents many times over the years that followed. It became a favourite and Calvin grew familiar with the twists and turns of the plot.

In this tale, a peasant does a good turn for an old lady, lending her his donkey so that she can carry her load of firewood to her cottage high in the mountains. She repays him by casting a spell on the beast so that it shits gold coins and will live for a hundred years.

The stupid peasant, however, sees only a reduction in the value of his donkey. Its dung is now no use to him as fertiliser on his cabbage patch because it is thick with pieces of shiny metal, and the stubborn creature becomes so lazy and self-important that it won't work for him.

Furthermore, the peasant can't even sell the donkey, for although the rich men of the town like the idea of an endless stream of gold, they are far too upstanding to handle donkey shit, and far too untrusting to have anyone filter the faeces for them. And anyway, the obstinate animal would not suffer itself to be led or dragged down the winding path to town and away from its comfortable and much loved stable in the corner of the peasant's field.

In the end, only a young lad is kind enough to look after the donkey, tending to its needs and bringing it fresh thistles and water. And only he is wise enough to realise that everything can be washed clean with enough soap and water, while all smells can be masked with sufficient lavender. He becomes the very rich companion of the

The Donkey with Golden Shit

donkey, and builds himself a fine house right next to the donkey's stall.

* * * * *

Young Calvin became quite obsessed with this fairy tale. Whenever he passed a donkey he would insist on checking its stools for gold. At first his parents laughed and thought this was sweet; but a foolish whim once encouraged soon becomes an unbreakable habit. And when Calvin started to sift shit through his finger, his elders realised things had got out of (or rather, into) hand.

But the best efforts of his elders did nothing more than make a strange behaviour into a closet secret activity. Calvin would sneak out at night to visit the stalls and fields. He kept careful lists in a code he had invented so that he knew which animals he had already checked.

By the time he was in his early teens, Calvin knew that it was none of the local donkeys that had magic poo. Faced with quartering the world in his search and examining every donkey dropping, he started to question everyone he met to see if they could help him with his quest.

"Have you seen the donkey that shits gold pieces?" he would ask. "Do you know where I can find it?"

The responses were not always helpful. Some people just laughed at him. Others gave crude answers relating to cows that pissed liquid gold. But a few took care to give him detailed directions to high pastures in the Aosta valley or to the dry hills of Umbria. Yet when Calvin returned dusty and disappointed, those same people

The Donkey with Golden Shit

were waiting and laughing.

* * * * *

Calvin turned into a withdrawn boy. He retreated into his studies and became a model student of the literature and folklore of his people. He soon found that all fairy tales contain a grain of truth and began a great collection. But always at the top of his mind was the story of the donkey and its golden shit.

He discovered that this story was a constant across the whole of Italy. There were many variations and it became a kind of hobby for him. When he started work as an accountant's assistant he travelled all over Italy to visit firms and help with audits. Each time he journeyed he would quiz the people he met about donkeys and the properties of their shit. Sometimes this was embarrassing for his colleagues. Sometimes people laughed at him. Sometimes there was confusion because surely the gold coins came out of the donkey's mouth when it brayed, or was it silver pieces that fell from its ears when you pulled its tail? But over time Calvin built up quite a collection of donkey tales that he had scribbled down in his notebook in different parts of the country.

Calvin moved from job to job. No one really wanted a mediocre trainee accountant whose mind was not on the job and who could surprise even the most refined client by suddenly enquiring about the local donkey population and the likelihood of becoming rich by running your fingers through the locally-produced donkey shit.

Then, finding himself between jobs and trying to make a bowl of soup last all day and serve as both a late breakfast and early supper, Calvin bemoaned his fate to

The Donkey with Golden Shit

the owner of the small café where he was sheltering from the grey day.

"Would that I could just find that donkey," he said. "Of course, I know it is just a story, but it would be wonderful. No more financial problems, no more having to work for an uninterested and uninteresting master, and the only drawback solved with a little soap and water."

"You know so much about donkey shit," said the proprietor, who had heard it all before, "that you should be a professor. And will Mister Professor Asscrap be wanting anything else this evening, or can I take away that bowl before you scrape the pattern off?"

"But why not?" thought Calvin. I bet the Department of Cultural History would be interested. Or maybe the Faculty of Peasant Studies. Or I could speak with the Dean of Antiquities in Rural Development.

As it happened, Calvin had to have more than a few conversations and interviews before he found the right person to understand his proposal. He was passed between the Department of Veterinary Science and the Professor of Comparative Zoology. He spent time at the University of Alternative Crop Husbandry and made a special trip to the Institute of Folk Art on the mistaken idea that he planned to sculpt statues of animals out of only their own faeces.

But finally he secured a place as a doctoral student in a small college dedicated to research into psychology and literature. Those who knew him were unsure whether he was doing research in his own right or was the subject of someone else's experiment.

* * * * *

The Donkey with Golden Shit

Writing a thesis turned out to be easy for Calvin. He had already read nearly all of the background material, he had his own extensive research notes, and he was the uncontested expert in his field.

Progressing his work required little more than advancing his own theories of categorisation, and publishing a few papers on the psychology of dreams: dreams of wealth, dreams of something for nothing, dreams of shit, and dreams of forming lifelong bonds with animals. Some professors in Austria were particularly avid readers, and it was probably on the strength of this audience that his own university granted him a doctorate, although they may have been influenced by the smell of excrement emanating from his office in a remote corner of the campus.

And so, although considered mad by everyone in the faculty, Doctor Di Allegori left the university as a man of letters and resumed his quest for a job. But he found that even where his prior reputation was forgotten or unknown, his doctorate did not earn him any respect. For when he had to answer the question, "Oh, a Learned Doctor, that is impressive. What was the title of your thesis?" he would be forced to answer, "On an Understanding of the Origins of Excrement of Immense Value in the genus Equus Africanus Asinus," and that was usually enough to guarantee that someone else got the job or else that the vacancy was no longer in immediate need of filling.

Indeed, Calvin's reputation as "an eccentric" preceded him at every turn. Jobs seemed to elude him the way his special donkey had done, and he was forced to live a pauper's life scratching a living writing pieces for the Donkey Breeders' Gazette.

The Donkey with Golden Shit

Sitting in his single-room apartment under the eaves of the loft above a haberdasher's shop, Calvin moved his papers around to avoid the drips from the leaking roof. But he managed to bring some stability and calmness to his life by working on what he thought might be the definitive version of the fairy story. Over many months, sustained only by dry bread and watery cabbage soup, Calvin wrote and rewrote his manuscript. He polished the text and drew on ideas from the many different versions of the tale that he had collected over the years.

Finally, when he thought it was as perfect as it could be, he started to take it around publishers. At a cost that he could hardly afford, he made copies and sent them to magazines and journals around the world. But at best he received the occasional polite rejection. Mainly, he was ignored. Sometimes he got a more clear answer, epitomised by the response from the Commissioning Editor of The Children's Library, a specialist publishing house operating out of Modena. It read:

> Dear S. Di Allegori,
> We are in receipt of your manuscript, but we must ask: who wants to read a story about donkey shit? That's a crap idea.

From then onwards, Calvin slipped into a decline. He was rapidly dismissed from the few jobs he did manage to find, either for talking to the customers about the different kinds of donkey to be found in Italy, which was not so bad, but then continuing to describe their faecal matter, or for spending his working hours and his employers' stationery making endless revisions to his tale.

The Donkey with Golden Shit

It was only after he had been buried in a pauper's grave that a young man found Calvin's story and was wise enough to recognize that it is not the publisher but the reader who is the judge of the merit of a tale. He built himself a printing press and became very rich from that donkey and its gold pieces.

The Inn at Chillingford

Yesterday evening, at half past six or thereabouts, as I was making my way home from the fields where I had been weeding the lilies, I was stopped by a bear who asked me, in the most courteous of words, if I wouldn't tell him the way to Chillingford and give him directions to the inn that is situated there.

Well, I didn't much like the sound of that: a bear drinking at an inn with the common people, and on a Sunday too. So I feigned ignorance, and told him I was unable to be of assistance.

"It is of no matter," said the bear. "Please don't distress yourself on my account. But allow me to walk with you a while as I have no better plan."

Well, it was only a moderately sized bear, certainly smaller than many I have met, but I did not wish to appear rude by refusing it in case it insisted. So we walked on together, from time to time pointing out interesting features of the scenery to each other and discussing the market price of livestock and especially fish.

After a while we came to a fork in the road and the bear sat down on the milestone to decide which way he would go.

I noticed a rich crop of wild berries nearby and began to graze upon them. This gave the bear an idea and, pulling a string bag from his pocket, he set about picking the fruits and collecting them in that receptacle.

"These," he informed me, "will make an excellent cordial that I can take to my grandmother."

After a time, when his bag was bulging full, the bear bade me good day and set off on one path. I, following the signpost to Chillingford, selected the other and, on reaching the town, made my way to the inn where I took a few drinks to steady my nerves.

Goodman's Rock

On the high moor, far above the pasture and hayfields, on the land grazed by summer sheep and speckled with spring flowers and haunted by children scavenging for winberries in the autumn, sits a large slab of limestone known as Goodman's Rock.

It seems curiously out of place on the peatbog that is underlaid with rough sandstone and millstone grit. Yet there it is, solid and flat like a giant's coffee table or an altar, or maybe a place of ritual sacrifice used by the ancients.

Many tales are told about Goodman's Rock. Ghost stories to send children to bed with an extra chill on cold winter's nights. Love stories for balmy summer evenings. Fairy tales for the gullible and simple-minded. But, truth be told, no one really knows how Goodman's Rock came to be there where the wind whistles through the coarse grasses and the curlew pines wistfully for better times. Nor does anyone know how it got its name or even who the good man may have been.

* * * * *

Tom Palmer had always loved it up there at Goodman's Rock. He revelled in the noise that the silence left in his ears. He liked the view of the distant plain and the cottages laid out below him. And he was quite at home with the sun and wind in his face or the rain and snow lashing his back. It was why he was happy with his job shepherding the ragged sheep that grazed the tops.

Most of all Tom liked to sit on Goodman's Rock and eat his lunch, or stand on it to survey the land around and check on his flock. On sunny days he would stretch himself out, his feet hanging off the end of the slab, his

Goodman's Rock

harms hanging one off each side, and stare up into the deep blue that was dotted by skylarks or sliced across by the paths of rooks. Sometimes a sparrowhawk would rip the air as it passed, and on the days before a change in the weather white gulls would circle, lost without the sea on which to settle.

* * * * *

One afternoon, not long after the flock had been turned out for the first time in a new year, Tom heard a frantic bleating as he approached the rock. Was one of his charges in trouble? He broke into a trot as he climbed the last few hundred feet to the summit where the stone sat, and the cries seemed to get louder as he got closer to the rock. But search though he did, he couldn't find the distressed animal anywhere, and when he jumped up on to the rock itself to get a better view of the surrounding land the bleating stopped as suddenly as it had started.

A few weeks later, or perhaps several months had passed and it was getting close to gathering time for the shearers to do their hot work, as the long summer evening was turning to dusk, Tom could have sworn he caught the sound of moaning brought to him on the breeze. Was someone hurt? Perhaps a tripper from the market town out for a day in the sunshine had twisted an ankle and fallen somewhere. He listened carefully to get a bearing on the distressed voice and then followed the guidance of his ears.

In no time he was at Goodman's Rock, but had seen no one. So he climbed on to the platform and cried out, "Who is there? Are you hurt?" But all at once the moaning stopped and the moor's evening silence settled around him.

Goodman's Rock

Then again, in the late golden days when the children roamed the hills with blue lips and tongues, their jugs brimming with the wild harvest, Tom's walk amongst his sheep was interrupted by the sound of sobbing. Quite distinct it was. Obviously some infant had fallen victim to the taunts of its friends or had upset its haul of winberries. Up Tom climbed again towards his favourite perch, calling out, "Don't you be worrying about a thing, now. Tom's on his way and he'll put everything right." But Tom just could not find where the child was hidden, and when he hopped up on top of Goodman's Rock to get a better view, the sobbing gave way to silence. Perhaps, thought Tom, the children were playing a trick on him, taking advantage of his good nature to get a little sport. Well, at least no one was in trouble.

That year Tom was late bringing the sheep down off the mountain. He never could say why he left it until the frosts were riming the brown bracken fronds. It may have been to get a little extra grazing off the land and so make the winter feed last a bit better, or it might have been that his mind was occupied with thoughts of Mary Wright who had become a whole lot more interesting over the last six months. Anyway, Tom crunched his way through frozen grass and stood atop Goodman's Rock to get a last sighting of the land and to see if he could spot any stragglers who had avoided the gathering.

As he stood there filling his lungs with cold air, a whispering voice came to him quite clearly. "Trapped," it said. "Oh, the weight of stone on my poor body. Will I ever get free or am I destined to rot here? Is there no hope for me?"

Tom was quite taken aback and stood stock still until he was quite sure that his ears were not playing him for a fool. Then, moving quietly and softly he lowered

Goodman's Rock

himself to the ground and walked around the rock once or twice. Yes, the voice was coming from under the stone.

He spoke up bravely. "I can hear you, you know," he said. "Are you stuck under the rock? How do you come to be there?"

With barely a pause the voice continued bemoaning its fate. "Trapped," it repeated, "pressed down flat by this huge slab. Never able to move at all. Can no one get me out from under this weight?"

"Well," spoke up Tom, "I can't be doing anything with my bare hands, but if you can hold on for a bit I'll nip down to my hut and come back with a spade. Then we'll see what's what.

"Mind you," he added, "I still don't rightly see how you got yourself under there in the first place."

"Oh do please hurry." the voice implored him. "To be stuck like this on such a cold and clear night is more than I can bear."

Now, Tom knew the paths on the moor, and he knew the quickest routes. So it wasn't so long until he was back at Goodman's Rock with a spade in one hand and a sturdy iron bar in the other.

"Are you still there?" he cried.

"Oh," was the response, "the boy has a fine wit! Did you think I had just raised this rock and crawled out and away? I assure you I would not do such a thing. Not after I had put you to all the trouble of fetching a spade."

So Tom set to with his spade, cutting and lifting the peat along the long edge of the rock. He found the stone was quite thick: thicker than he would have guessed. The peat must have built up over long years, but about a foot down he hit sandstone. The whole block of Goodman's Rock was sitting flat and smooth on top of the sandstone bed.

"Are you sure you're under there?" he asked.

"As sure as a body can be when it has a weight of limestone pressing down on it. Do try to see if you can break through."

So Tom set to with his iron bar, chipping away at the sandstone where it supported the mass of Goodman's Rock. Slowly, over the space of an hour, as his iron bar clanged into the night, Tom managed to undermine a little hole and suddenly the bar shot forward and down into a void.

"Hey!" came a disgruntled shout. "Watch what you are at! I've not been lying here half squashed by a rock just so you can skewer me through with your lump of rusty metal."

Tom withdrew the bar and heard deep breaths from below the stone. The type of inhalations that a man might make on leaving the chicken shed after mucking out for an hour, or that a fellow would relish after sitting vigil with his father's corpse all night.

"That's better," came a sigh. "So much better. Come close to the hole and let me see if I can see my rescuer."

So Tom laid down the bar and stepped up to the rock, and quick as lightning a hand shot out of the hole and grabbed him round the ankle. He felt nails or claws dig into his flesh

"Don't stop now. Don't leave me here. You have to get me out. It would be too cruel to dash my hopes."

"Oh, but I must rest a while," Tom replied. "This is hard work and there's a deal more to be done."

"Well I ain't letting go of you now I've gotten you," the voice told him. "You're my escape and I won't let you run off and desert me."

Goodman's Rock

"There's no risk of that," were Tom's words of reassurance. "I said I'd get you out and I'm a man of my word."

"If you swear it then, that'll be all right. You can sit on the edge of the stone and rest. I can bear a little extra weight for a bit. But I isn't letting go."

So Tom made as solemn a promise as he had ever made and sat himself down to gather his strength.

"While we're here," he said, "and since neither of us is going anywhere, why don't you tell me the story of how you come to be stuck under this rock?"

"Since you gave your word so solemnly, and since you are just sat there, and since it has been so long since I talked with anyone, I don't think it will do any harm.

"Very many years ago, when the world was still new, I was as free as anything. I ran in the dawn with the hare, and faster I was. I flitted in sunlight with the butterfly, and lighter I was. I swam with the otter, and always it was I who caught the fish.

"But I was misunderstood by man. If I bathed in the spring and later the water turned brackish, was I to blame? If I danced in the pasture to the song of the moonlight, did that account for the cows yielding up sour milk? If I blew a merry tune on my pipe in the night, why blame me if the babies cried and the old men couldn't sleep? And when it was cold, who could blame me for lighting a small fire to stave off the chill? I never meant to burn down even one barn, and certainly not the church.

"And I always made a point of paying my debts. If I eased my hunger on a pie left to cool on a windowsill, why, then I would be glad to spend the afternoon and night looking after the child, taking it on a long walk down by the river or up here on the bog. If a fox got in with the chickens, I was always there to chase it around until in its frenzy it finally ran away, and I made sure it never carried off more than one of the birds it killed.

"In truth, I was picked on and maligned. People said I caused havoc just because I dislodged the soot from their chimneys. Well, it they had not locked and barred all of the doors and windows, I would not have had to come in that way. Then they said I caused the crops to fail, but that is silly. I did nothing that year except sit in the sun with the young girls from the village and make them happy by keeping the clouds out of the sky. They even blamed me the year the river froze hard and the water butts burst, but I know that the children loved the snow and delighted in the ice on the trees.

"And then one year a band of wicked men got together to hunt me down. The last straw, they said, was when their grain store got wet and the whole harvest rotted. You and I know that that is an essential step in making the ale they all loved, but did they thank me? No, they hunted me with silver! They even melted down the candlestick from the parson's own bedchamber to tip their arrows. And so I fled to the moorland.

"And what was I supposed to eat up here so far from the ovens and larders? All there is to be had is grass and sheep. But I didn't want to deprive the poor shepherds of their livelihoods, so I only ate the little ones. Just the tiny lambs that surely no one would miss.

"Perhaps I would still be free if it hadn't been for the interference of Hugh Goodman. Of course, he was no more a good man than I am an evil sprite. But he took them all in with his schemes and his plans and his books of learning. He it was who had this block of limestone quarried and dragged up the hill. He it was who measured out the pit they dug and in which I am trapped. And all the while I watched from a distance, keen to help with their work, but unable to get close because of the charms he had set around the place. And it was Hugh Goodman who baited the trap with a sow and her eight piglets.

"Not that they weren't tasty, but four hundred years is a long time when you only have a few pig bones to suck. And now I must get out. It has been so long since I tickled a goat to keep it amused while it was being milked, or told a joke to a carthorse to distract it when it was being shod, or helped the woodsman by pushing over the tree he was sawing through. So you understand why I can't let you go now that you have started to rescue me."

Tom sat quiet through this tale of sorrow, but now he spoke up. "It seems to me you have been badly used. No one should be so harshly punished for a few mistakes they make while trying to be helpful."

"I knew you were a good and kind-hearted fellow," came the voice from under the rock.

"But there is a problem," Tom explained. "I can't enlarge this hole or break in without some more tools and things. In fact, I think I need to fetch my horse and some rope, and a big lever, and some good stones to build a fulcrum. You'll have to trust me and let me go. I know you are desperate and have been ill-treated, but it is the only way."

"Then you will have to give me something to hold on trust: something that will bind you to me and ensure you come back. Why, of course! If you just pass me that ring, the one in your waistcoat pocket, the one you have been keeping to give to pretty young Miss Mary. Why, if you were to pass that down to me I should know you would be sure to return."

And when Tom passed the ring in, the clawed hand let go of his ankle and he stepped back.

Goodman's Rock

As quick as he could, Tom made his way home and was soon back leading his horse that pulled a cart loaded with blocks of good limestone, bars of iron, wood, and all sorts.

First he lit a big fire so that he could see what he was doing. Then he started to lay out the stone blocks. Then he built a kind of iron cage around Goodman's Rock, bolting all of the pieces of metal together firmly.

"What are you up to?" whined the voice, and the hand waved around frantically from the hole. "Come closer so I can touch your skin and know your plans."

"No time, no time," called Tom as he dashed about. "Too busy. Soon have this stone up."

Tom harnessed the horse to stout ropes tied to the metal around the rock. Then, almost as an afterthought, he set up a kettle over the fire, took one last look at the set-up, took a lever in both hands, and cried, "Walk on," to his horse.

For a moment nothing seemed to happen. The ropes creaked but nothing moved. Then, as Tom put his full weight on the lever, Goodman's Rock began to lift at one end. Ever so slightly at first, but then the gap grew. Bit by bit it widened: a crack, a sliver, a notch.

"Ah, good man," came the voice. "Soon. Soon."

First one hand, and then the other poked out, long nails scrabbling in the peat.

"Almost there. Just a little wider, and I'll squeeze through."

But, "No further, cursed boggle!" cried Tom, dropping the lever and drawing his knife to cut the rope.

Goodman's Rock came crashing down, leaving just a pair of gnarled hands severed and twitching on the moor.

Tom set to with stone and iron, building up and over Goodman's Rock until it was a great construction

153

twice as high and twice as wide as it had ever been. Then, taking the kettle from the fire, he poured an elaborate pattern of molten silver over the mound and into the cracks.

    When he was quite done, Tom loaded the cart with what was left and hitched up his horse. Stooping for a moment, he picked up the two gory relics, slipped the ring from one of the fingers and tossed the hands on to the fire.

* * * * *

On the high moor, far above the pasture and hayfields, on land grazed by summer sheep, stands a huge mound of limestone intertwined with iron and silver called Palmer's Folly. Many tales are told about how this mound came to be there, but truth be told, no one really knows how Palmer's Folly came to be there where the wind whistles through the coarse grasses and the curlew pines wistfully for better times. Nor does anyone know how it got its name or even who or what Palmer was.

Feathers

There was a boy who used to collect feathers.

Whenever he saw one he would pick it up and carry it back to his room.

He had deep black crow feathers and iridescent peacock feathers. He had red down from a robin's breast, and snowy wisps from the chest of an owl.

If you had asked him why he did it, he might have said, "They are so beautiful," or, "It is a shame to leave them out in the rain to rot."

One day the boy had collected so many feathers that he had a whole bird. He climbed on its back and together they flew off into the world.

Not Possible

Ferdinand was just eight years old. His birthday was in October and he had helped with the harvest for the third year in a row. He was now the eldest child in the family still at home: his eldest sister Rosanne had left to marry a potter in the big town beyond the hills; his big brother Joseph was in the King's army; and his favourite brother Jakob had left two years ago to travel down the river and find work on the rich farms on the plain where there was always a shortage of labour.

Now Ferdinand was the main help to his father, tending the goats on the scrubby pasture, milking their cow, and gathering the small harvest of oats and hay. He was also the chief assistant to his mother in fetching firewood, carrying pails of water, and kneading dough for the weekly bake of grey bread.

Four smaller children looked up to Ferdinand as a role model, a playmate, a safeguard, and a minor deity: Xavier the baby was like a new discovery for the family with his unexpected gurglings and strange gesticulations; Mary the toddler was into everything and invariably filthy; Elizabeth, at five years old, was everyone's darling with long curly blond hair; and Wilhelm tagged along behind Ferdinand admiring him the way Ferdinand had himself idolized Jakob.

One evening towards the end of October, after the smaller children had gone to bed, his parents sat Ferdinand down for a serious chat. Ferdinand knew it was important because his father fiddled with his unlit pipe while his mother wiped down the kitchen table for the second time.

"I think you know how bad the harvest was this year," his father said. "You have three younger brothers and a sister, and it is just not possible for us to feed all five

Not Possible

of you this winter. You must do what Joseph and Jakob did when you were little: you must leave home and seek your fortune in the wide world."

"You must not think we don't love you," his mother told him. "We love all of our children equally, but you're big enough to fend for yourself and it is simply not possible for you to stay here with us any longer."

"There will be frosts soon, so you need to head south as quickly as you can. The best thing you can do," his father declared, "is to pack your things and be on your way at first light before the little ones wake up. It's for the best and it's not possible to say goodbye to them without upsetting them needlessly."

Well, of course Ferdinand was upset. He wanted to know why these things were not possible and why his parents were unable to protect him.

His father was stern and explained how the world worked for people like them. "In this life, young Ferdinand, you will discover there are many things that are not possible. You must not be daunted by them and you must not be afraid. You must just learn to take what life throws at you and live with what comes your way, even the things that are not possible."

So the very next morning, carrying a small backpack with his spare clothes, a blanket, and a loaf of bread, and with his knife strapped to his belt, Ferdinand shook his father's hand, kissed his mother's cheek, and set off on the path toward the south.

Two days later, as he was passing through a great wood, Ferdinand heard someone sobbing. He made his way through the undergrowth and the crying got louder, but he couldn't find anyone. Looking around and under the trees he was about to give up his search when he realised it was actually one of the trees that was in tears.

Not Possible

Great drops of water dripped from its leaves and ran down its trunk. Shudders of grief shook every branch and root. "Surely," thought Ferdinand, "this is not possible."

But Ferdinand was filled with compassion and placed his hand on the bark of the tree's trunk. "Don't be sad," he said, just as he might have comforted a tearful Elizabeth. "Tell me what the matter is."

So the tree told him its story. How its friend and soulmate had been felled and turned into planks, and how its saplings had been hacked down by charcoal burners. And it thanked Ferdinand for taking the time to listen. "No other passer-by has bothered to hear my distress. Nobody believed a tree could be crying. To thank you for your kindness please take one of my branches and make yourself a sturdy staff, for your path ahead may be tiring."

The very next day, Ferdinand climbed up on to a rocky plateau. He leant heavily on his staff because the way up was steep and the air thin. When he reached flat ground he decided to take a break and seated himself with his back against a boulder to nibble some of his bread. Stretching out his arm, Ferdinand suddenly felt something warm and sticky under his fingers. He looked closely and saw blood. The stone was bleeding from a crack on its side. This, Ferdinand knew, was completely not possible.

As quickly as he could, the boy pressed soil into the crack and packed it with moss. Then he bound it tightly with bracken. It looked as though he had staunched the flow and the rock thanked him for his care. It explained how it had been injured when a careless giant had dropped it. "Many people have passed this way, but none of them helped me because they all knew that it is not possible for a rock to bleed. I would like to reward you for

Not Possible

your aid. Please roll me over and help yourself to precious gems you will find beneath me."

So Ferdinand resumed his journey, his pack a little heavier because of the bag of opals and rubies he had collected.

Before the day was out, Ferdinand came to the place where the course of the river left the plateau and descended in a series of falls into the valley below. But to his amazement he saw that the water was flowing uphill. Although this was not possible, it was clearly happening, and Ferdinand sat down by a pool on the edge of the plateau to watch.

Quite suddenly he became aware of a fish swimming around and around in the water. It kept attempting to swim downstream, only downstream was now upstream and it kept being swept back into the pool.

Ferdinand gathered leaves and grasses and soaked them as thoroughly as he could. Then he scooped the fish from the water, wrapped it up safely and carried it down the hill until he reached a place where the river was flowing the right way. There he carefully slipped the fish back into the water.

The fish was delighted. It explained that it needed to get all the way to the coast to spend the winter in the sea. There it would be warm and there would be plenty of food. "Many travellers passed my pool, but none paid attention to my plight. Who would believe that a stream could flow uphill? They all knew that was not possible.

"I would like to give you something in return for your help. Follow me along the bank. Do you see that herb growing by the edge of the water? Pick it and cherish it, for it is Hurtsbane and just a little of it will cure any fever and heal any wound."

Not Possible

After only a few more days Ferdinand could tell he was quite far south. The nights were warmer and he didn't shiver himself to sleep wrapped in his thin blanket each night. But he had another problem: he had finished his bread and he was quite without food.

Passing by a cottage, Ferdinand saw a fruit tree in the garden. The tree was laden with ripe cherries, apricots, and melons. Maybe this was not possible and certainly not in November, but he was so hungry he knew he simply must have some of the fruit.

But Ferdinand was well-brought-up and understood the importance of each person's own harvest. So he went to the door of the cottage and knocked. There was no answer so he went inside and called out. "Hello! I'm a passing journeyer in need of food. If I pick you some of the fruits from your tree, will you share them with me?" But still there was no answer, so he took a big bowl from the table and went back into the garden.

When Ferdinand had filled the bowl with all manner of ripe fruits he set it back on the table and, since there was still no one around, he turned his back on the cottage and went on his way. This was much harder than he thought it would be because his stomach growled at him, but he found it was possible.

He had hardly gone any distance when he met an old woman shrunken with age and bent nearly double over her walking stick. "Young man," she greeted him. "Thank you for your kindness. The branches of my tree are too high for me to reach so I can't pick my fruit. Yet everyone who passes assumes that it is not possible for such a bounty to be left on the tree without good reason, so I go without.

"To repay your efforts I would like to give you this small bag of candied fruits from my garden," she said. "It

Not Possible

may only be a little sack, but you will find that no matter how much you pull from it, it will always be full."

Ferdinand went on his way much fortified, but wondering when he would find a town or a farm where he could get work. Not much further along the path he came to a lake. Standing in the waters was a fine white mare. The sun shone off its coat and Ferdinand was sure he had never seen such a splendid horse. But as he got closer he saw that it stood with one hoof placed on a water lily flower. "What are you doing?" he called out to it.

"I'm trapped," the animal replied. "My hoof is quite firmly stuck in the petals of this flower. I can't go forwards or back."

Again Ferdinand was confronted with something he knew was not possible. But he took his knife, waded into the lake, and cut the bloom from around the horse's foot.

The creature was ecstatic. It cantered around on the shore neighing like a foal. "Oh, it is so good to be free! When people passed by they all said it was not possible that a fine mare like me would be abandoned. Some said it was a trick, others that I was a mirage. I am so grateful that I will accompany you on your journey and you can ride me: not all the time, of course, but when there is pressing need."

The very next day, the boy and the horse saw a farm in the distance and decided to try their luck for work and a dry stable. As they got closer they saw a man working in one of the fields and approached him to ask his advice. Much to his surprise Ferdinand saw that it was Jakob. He knew that that was not possible because his favourite brother had gone to work on the land in the west. But he wasn't about to reject his brother just because he couldn't possibly be there, and the two boys hugged each other fondly.

Not Possible

Jakob explained to Ferdinand that the farm was not a good place to work. The farmer beat the workers and never paid them. So he gathered his few possessions, shouldered his pitchfork, and set out with his younger brother.

Before long the brothers came across a huge urn standing at the side of the path. How it could have got there and what it was for was a mystery. Jakob idly tapped on the side and they were astonished when he was answered by frantic knocking and shouting from inside the vessel.

"That's not possible," Jakob declared, looking at the narrow top of the jar. "No one could have climbed in there."

But Ferdinand calmly replied that if life had taught him anything it was that things were sometimes possible even when they were not possible. And taking up his staff he smashed the pot to pieces.

There, lying in the rubble, was their sister Rosanne. She explained that her husband had tired of her, preferring a new and younger wife. So he trapped her in a pot of his own making and abandoned her.

The family continued on their way and met a stag standing on the path in front of them. It was a huge beast, at least as big as Ferdinand's horse. On its head, framed by its majestic antlers, was a mirror. The brothers and their sister knew this was not possible, but while the mare and the stag exchanged pleasantries about the location of good grazing, the three youngsters peered into the glass.

What they saw was a horrendous scene of battle. A man on a brown charger was surrounded by pikemen. He waved his sword valiantly, but they had him trapped with their long fierce weapons.

Not Possible

"Quickly, Joseph," cried Ferdinand, "jump through the mirror before it is too late."

Joseph rapidly assessed the situation and turned his horse towards safety. The animal needed no encouragement and cleared the distance in one bound.

Well, all four siblings were delighted to see each other again, the mare was rather pleased to have the company of a stallion, and the stag was just happy to help.

A little later, the four came across a rose bush. The branches had woven themselves into a cage, and trapped in the middle was a nightingale.

"This is not possible," lamented the bird. "How can I have been so stupid as to get caught like this?"

"The only thing that is not possible," Ferdinand told it, "is 'not possible' itself." And he leant forward and opened the door of the cage.

"You are very kind," said the nightingale. "But I must tell you some bad news. When I flew over your home earlier today I saw it was under attack from a griffin. You must hurry if you want to save your family."

So they mounted up, Rosanne behind Ferdinand on the mare, and Jakob and Joseph on the charger. And they rode like the wind.

Back at their farmstead all was in chaos. The young children were hiding in the empty root store and the griffin sat in the smouldering ruins of the house. In one claw it held the body of their father while with the other it tried to defend itself from their mother who was wielding a mop with all her fury.

The warhorse charged straight in. While Jakob pinned the monster to the ground with his pitchfork, Joseph drew his sword and hacked its head off. Rosanne took out the Hurtsbane and before he knew it their father was hale and hearty again. Then the family had a good meal from the fruit bag, the first proper food some of them had had in a good long time.

"But what shall we do now?" asked Wilhelm, surveying the smoking debris of the house. "Surely it is not possible to rebuild our home."

"For once I agree," chuckled Ferdinand. "Some things really are not possible. But don't worry. I have more than enough money in these gemstones. We can buy ourselves a new house on a good farm with enough land to feed us all."

And unless something that is not possible has happened to them, that is exactly where they are all living today.

Tales from the Wood

by Adrian Farrel

Tales from the Wood is Adrian Farrel's first collection of fairy stories. Containing eighteen original tales, this anthology revisits some of our favourite and best-known stories from our childhoods, but presents them with a new twist and a different perspective. So we hear from Hansel and Gretel's father, we learn the true story of Pretty Blue Cloak and her dealings with the wolf, and we encounter the Stonecutter's Daughter tasked with spinning straw into gold.

Also in this collection you can meet The Princesses with Hairy Hands, The Clever Little Tailor, and Peter Pretzel who has his feet on backwards.

More Tales from the Wood

by Adrian Farrel

If you are enchanted by the stories in *Tales from the Wood* then you will want to read a collection of a further eighteen tales from the same author.

In *More Tales from the Wood* you can meet the Foxwife, the Fisherman and Findo Gask. You can visit the Chocolate Shop and the Toy Box. And you can step into the worlds of Freckly Freda, the Little Mermaid, and the Ugly Pumpkin.

Each new fairy tale is crafted with as much care and love as those in *Tales from the Wood*, and each has its own unusual twist or presents a view from an unexpected direction.

Tales from the Castle

by Adrian Farrel

If you have enjoyed the stories in *Tales from the Wood*, *More Tales from the Wood*, and *Tales from Beyond the Wood* then you can continue by reading the next collection of fairy tales from the same author.

With *Tales from the Castle* Adrian Farrel continues to deliver original fairy stories. This collection takes his readers inside the walls of the castle and up on to the battlements to look out over the fields and woodland towards the distant ocean. Here you can read about Grandfather Mercurius and find out how he outstayed his welcome, you can travel with Moshe and Kidda as they discover the value of foresight, and you can go shopping with Mary and a monster.

No words were hurt in the production of these tales. All writing was carefully monitored by the Authors' Humane Associaton.

About the Author

Adrian Farrel is a grandfather, father, and husband.

Before this departure into fairy stories, his writing was limited to technical reference books and to specifications for Internet protocols. Those, too, in some sense have an element of truth running through them.

Adrian divides his life between North Wales and the Alps. He works in the telecommunications industry to make the Internet function better and still spends more time worrying about the politics and social impact of the Internet than is reasonable.

You can find him on Twitter as @llanolddog

He blogs about his tales and fairy stories in general on his Facebook page TalesFromTheWood.